P9-APD-960

Enjoy all of these American Girl Mysteries®:

THE SILENT STRANGER   A *Kaya* Mystery

LADY MARGARET'S GHOST   A *Felicity* Mystery

SECRETS IN THE HILLS   A *Josefina* Mystery

THE RUNAWAY FRIEND   A *Kirsten* Mystery

SHADOWS ON SOCIETY HILL   An *Addy* Mystery

THE CRY OF THE LOON   A *Samantha* Mystery

A THIEF IN THE THEATER   A *Kit* Mystery

CLUES IN THE SHADOWS   A *Molly* Mystery

THE TANGLED WEB   A *Julie* Mystery

and many more!

— A *Samantha* MYSTERY —

THE CRY
OF THE LOON

by Barbara Steiner

Published by American Girl Publishing, Inc.
Copyright © 2009 by American Girl, LLC
All rights reserved. No part of this book may be used or
reproduced in any manner whatsoever without written
permission except in the case of brief quotations embodied
in critical articles and reviews.

Questions or comments? Call 1-800-845-0005, visit our
Web site at **americangirl.com**, or write to Customer Service,
American Girl, 8400 Fairway Place, Middleton, WI 53562-0497.

Printed in China
09 10 11 12 13 14 LEO 10 9 8 7 6 5 4 3 2 1

All American Girl marks, American Girl Mysteries®,
Samantha®, Samantha Parkington®, Nellie™, and Nellie O'Malley™
are trademarks of American Girl, LLC.

The characters and events portrayed in this book are fictitious. Any similarity
to real persons, living or dead, is coincidental and not intended.

PICTURE CREDITS
The following individuals and organizations have generously
given permission to reprint illustrations contained in "Looking Back":
pp. 174–175—lake scene, James Randklev/Getty Images; bathing beauties,
Bettmann/Corbis; pp. 176–177—Mirror Lake Inn, Cosmo Condina/Getty Images;
loons, © Arthur Morris/Corbis; hunters and campers, photo by
J.F. Holley, courtesy of the Adirondack Museum; pp. 178–179—ticket,
courtesy Larry Miller collection; steamer, photo by Edward Bierstadt, courtesy
Larry Miller collection; striped tent, courtesy of the Adirondack Museum;
W.W. Durant, courtesy of the Adirondack Museum; The Main Lodge at Great
Camp Sagamore, photo by Dave Scranton; pp. 180–181—map, courtesy of the
Adirondack Museum; sign post, photo by Jimmy S. Emerson, DVM;
hikers, © Carl Heilman II/Wild Visions, Inc.

Illustrations by Jean-Paul Tibbles

Cataloging-in-Publication Data
available from the Library of Congress.

For my granddaughter, Meghan Kane,
the toughest, hardest-working girl I know

TABLE OF CONTENTS

1
A BAD OMEN

The little steamboat sounded a mournful hoot as it approached the dock at Piney Point. Fingers of fog slipped under Samantha's coat collar, making her shiver. Wispy clouds circled Samantha and Nellie like ghosts. It seemed as if the girls had left summer behind in New York City. Nellie, Samantha's adopted sister and very best friend, was nervous on the water. She clutched Samantha's arm so tightly that surely her fingers made dents in Samantha's skin.

"Are you here at last, girls?" a familiar voice boomed from the foggy shore.

Samantha giggled, feeling safe. "Yes, Admiral," she called. "It's us." Nellie relaxed her grip.

Samantha took a deep breath of the pine-scented air. Oh, how she loved coming to Piney Point. The dampness and mist brought out the rich smells of earth and trees. She always wished that she could bottle the smells, take them home to New York City, and open the bottle whenever she missed the woods.

Thump. The boat bumped the wooden dock. The steam engine hissed softly, leaving the girls surrounded by an eerie quiet. Then a trembling wail filled the air.

Ooo–oooo, ooo–oooo, ooo–oooo ooo–oooo.

"What's that?" Nellie whispered, clutching Samantha's arm again. Their younger sisters gathered close, too.

"Is it a ghost, Samantha?" Jenny grabbed Samantha's other arm.

"Or an evil spirit?" Bridget asked. She'd been reading scary stories before they left New York. Samantha hoped she'd left them behind and brought something cheerful to read, like *Heidi.*

"No," Samantha said. "It's a bird called a loon." Samantha loved the loon's cry, but she had to admit it sounded spooky in the fog.

A Bad Omen

"I never heard a birdcall like that," Nellie said. She kept her hold on Samantha's arm.

"Loons live here on the lake," Samantha explained. "The same pair come back every year to make a nest and have their babies. Wait until you see the babies riding on the mother's back."

Jenny giggled and looked ready to ask another question. But just then Hildy Stewart joined them at the boat railing. Hildy was the new maid that Aunt Cornelia had hired to accompany the girls from New York City and to help Grandmary at Piney Point.

"I hope I won't be sorry I came here," Hildy murmured. She peered doubtfully at the shore-line cloaked with towering dark pines. Samantha thought that Hildy looked very young, but she remembered all the stories Nellie had told of girls—children, really—working in mills and factories. Being a maid was a much better job and certainly less dangerous.

"Wait till the sun comes out," Samantha said. "The lodge and the woods are beautiful. On your day off, you can swim in the lake and hike—"

Hildy shook her head. "I've never gone swimming, or hiking, either. Is there a town nearby?"

Samantha didn't answer Hildy's question. She didn't want to tell her the truth—that there was no place to go unless you took this ferryboat back across Goose Lake to the little village they'd set off from an hour ago.

From the mound of baggage that the steward was piling near the railing, Hildy picked up her suitcase and a hatbox, ready to get off the boat. Samantha lifted her own suitcase and a colorfully wrapped box with a big red bow. The box held a gift for Grandmary's birthday, which was only a few days away. The gift was from Uncle Gard and Aunt Cornelia, who'd had to stay home this summer because of their new baby. Samantha missed them already.

The sight of the Admiral hurrying down the dock cheered her up. "Welcome to Piney Point, girls!" He stretched out a hand, helped Samantha step across to the dock, and wrapped her in a hug. Then he helped the other three girls and Hildy. He lifted a suitcase in each hand.

A BAD OMEN

"Come on," he said. "Let's go up to the lodge and say hello to Grandmary."

"I can hardly wait to see her," Samantha said.

"She's eager to see you, too. How's that new baby, William Samuel?" The Admiral laughed. "That's a big name for a tiny baby."

Samantha had thought the same thing when she'd first seen the red-faced, squalling newborn. Uncle Gard and Aunt Cornelia said they'd named him after Grandfather and Samantha. Of course, they couldn't name a boy Samantha, so they'd chosen Samuel.

"You aren't going to call him Sam, are you?" Samantha had asked Uncle Gard. She liked having the baby named after her, but she wasn't sure she wanted to share the special nickname that Uncle Gard had for her.

"I expect we'll call the baby William," Uncle Gard had said. Uncle Gard held the baby a lot. Samantha thought that was sweet. She wondered if her own father had held her and looked at her as lovingly when she was a baby.

"Uncle Gard says William will grow into

his name," Samantha told the Admiral.

"I'm sure he will—and faster than we can imagine," said the Admiral. "It's grand to see you girls, Samantha. We've had a lot of bad weather, but now that you're here, I know the sun will come out, and it won't be so gloomy." He turned to a man approaching them on the dock. "Get an armful of luggage, Jim. These girls have brought half of New York City with them." There was laughter behind the Admiral's words. Samantha always knew when he was teasing her.

In the dim light, she recognized the Admiral's friend, Trapper Jim. The tall, thin man might have seemed unfriendly had she not met him the last time she was at Piney Point. He took her suitcase from her hand to carry up the hill.

"Thank you, Jim. I'm so glad to see you," Samantha said. "You and the Admiral haven't been fishing while you waited, have you?"

"No fishing, Samantha. We fished yesterday, though."

"Meet my new sisters, Jim—Nellie, Bridget, and Jenny." Shortly after Samantha had gone to

live with Uncle Gard and Aunt Cornelia, they
had adopted Samantha's best friend, Nellie, and
her younger sisters, Bridget and Jenny. Nellie
and her sisters had lost their parents to influenza.

As they all left the dock and started up the
path toward the house, Samantha told her sisters
that Trapper Jim was a hunting and fishing guide
who worked around the lakes and mountains.
He and the Admiral had become good friends
last summer. Samantha had enjoyed hearing him
tell wonderful stories of the mountains before so
many city people had built summer homes on
the lakes.

Jim's face was brown and full of lines, like
very old leather. He had a large beak of a nose,
and his hair was snow white. He reminded
Samantha of a majestic bald eagle she had once
seen at Piney Point. Jim carried himself with
that same sense of pride, as if he owned these
mountains.

The Admiral said that everyone in the mountains knew Jim and liked hunting with him. Now
that he was getting older, Jim worked as a guide

only when he needed extra money. Samantha knew he much preferred spending time with people he liked, including Admiral Archibald Beemis, Grandmary's husband.

Ooo–oooo, ooo–oooo, ooo–oooo. The loon yodeled again, interrupting Samantha's thoughts.

"Are those birds going to make that sound all the time?" Hildy asked. She glanced back through the dripping pines toward the dock as if she already wished she could leave. A slight wind had picked up, ruffling the water into choppy waves. Samantha looked back the way they had come. She had never seen the lake look so uninviting.

Jim cast an amused glance at Hildy. "Loons have lived here longer than any of us can imagine. All through the North Country, many stories are told about loons. The Cree Indians thought the cry came from a lonely warrior trying to find his way into heaven."

"Goodness," Nellie said. "That's sad."

"Go ahead, Jim," the Admiral said, juggling his load of luggage. "Tell them all the tales."

Samantha smiled. She remembered from last summer that Jim loved telling spooky stories. She'd gotten used to them, but now he had a new audience.

In a quiet voice, Jim went on. "The Chippewa Indians thought the cry of the loon was an omen of death."

"Oh, Samantha." Bridget moved closer to Samantha and Nellie. "Is someone going to die?"

"Of course not, Bridget." Samantha had heard the legend before, but it still gave her shivers. She hugged her little sister. "That's just a superstition. Let's hurry and find Grandmary."

Suddenly two eerie hoots came from the woods. *Ooo . . . oooo*. Samantha jumped. Jenny and Bridget clutched her arms again. That was no loon call. What was it?

Then laughter burst through the trees as a quavering voice moaned, "We're gho-o-osts, wandering Piney Point." Two boys, maybe thirteen or fourteen, emerged from the woods.

Samantha let out the breath she was holding. "Who are you?" she demanded, hands on her hips, angry that she'd let the boys frighten her.

"Jack," said the taller, dark-haired boy.

"Homer," said the red-haired boy. "Our pa works here. He sent us down to help you." The boys took some luggage from the Admiral and Jim and sped up the path.

"Is that true?" Samantha asked the Admiral after the boys were out of earshot. "Those boys work at Piney Point?"

"I'm afraid so," the Admiral said. "Your grandmother had to hire a new manager this summer. Those boys are part of the package."

The boys reminded Samantha of Eddie Ryland, the pesky boy who lived next door to Grandmary in Mount Bedford—the boy who had tried to ruin her birthday party when she turned ten. Her heart sank. Samantha wanted Nellie, Bridget, and Jenny to love Piney Point as much as she did.

Those two boys were not a good omen for the summer.

2
A TERRIBLE POSSIBILITY

Samantha and Nellie hurried to the top of the path. There they saw a large building made of logs, nestled among the pine trees.

"Is that *our* house?" Nellie stared. "That's not a cabin! I was imagining a tiny place. That's a— a mansion in the woods."

"It's not fancy, but there's room for our whole family," Samantha said, smiling. She hadn't told Nellie how big the lodge was so that Nellie would be surprised.

Grandmary waved to them from the porch. "There you are. Did you girls have a good trip on the train and the steamboat, despite the weather?"

"The trip was fine, Grandmary." Samantha ran up the steps and hugged her grandmother. "And we're here at last."

Grandmary turned to Hildy Stewart. "You must be Hildy. Welcome to Piney Point. I hope you'll like it here. It isn't always so gloomy."

Hildy curtsied. "Thank you, ma'am. I hope so, too."

"Samantha, you and Nellie will be sharing a bedroom this summer, as will Bridget and Jenny. Why don't you take the girls upstairs and see if you can guess which rooms are yours? Hildy, you can help the girls unpack later. Mrs. Hawkins needs help in the kitchen now."

Samantha watched the Admiral and Jim disappear inside with the luggage. "Come on, Nellie. You, too, Bridget and Jenny. I can't wait to show you around." She led the way inside the lodge.

The big living room was just as Samantha remembered. Large windows, framed by red curtains, let in lots of light. A cheerful fire burned in the huge stone fireplace along the north wall. Above it, an enormous moose head was mounted over the mantel, along with an old pair of snowshoes for decoration, one on either side.

A Terrible Possibility

A big sofa piled with pillows sat near the fireplace, with two rocking chairs close by. Samantha had loved sitting by the fire on rainy days last summer, reading or just daydreaming.

The crackling fire was tempting, as Samantha still felt shivery from the trip across the lake, but she wanted to see their rooms.

At the top of the stairs, Jenny ran ahead, peeking into every doorway until she exclaimed, "Look, there's a dollhouse. This must be our room, Bridget."

Samantha glanced into the room to see the dollhouse, which looked just like a tiny version of the lodge. She laughed to see a carved moose peering into one of the miniature windows. The Admiral must have built the dollhouse, and maybe Jim had helped.

Nellie called from another room. "This must be ours, Samantha! We have our own beds, and wicker chairs with cushions where we can sit and read."

Samantha ran to join her. One bedspread was blue, the other dark red. A blue and red braided

13

rug lay on the floor between the beds. "We'll have our own bathroom, too." Samantha showed Nellie the tiny room between the two bedrooms. "There's even running water." She turned the tap over a basin but nothing happened. Puzzled, she tried the tap again. "Well, there's *supposed* to be water. The lodge has two other bathrooms, too—one for Grandmary and the Admiral and a smaller one in back for Hildy and Mrs. Hawkins."

"I thought we'd have an outdoor bathroom," Nellie said with a grin.

"Come on, Nellie—let's go down to the kitchen and say hello to Mrs. Hawkins." Samantha and Nellie went back downstairs, leaving Bridget and Jenny to play with the dollhouse.

The kitchen smelled of roasting meat, fresh bread, and pies. "We're here, Mrs. Hawkins!" Samantha said as she ran to hug the woman who was almost a mother to her.

Mrs. Hawkins, smelling of cinnamon, gave Samantha a squeeze. "Oh, Samantha, I'm so glad to see you and Nellie. Girls, this is Glenda

Griffith." Mrs. Hawkins gestured toward a small, plump woman working at the big iron stove. "Her husband is the new manager. Glenda has already been so much help to me."

Mrs. Griffith smiled at Samantha and Nellie. Her dark eyes studied both girls before she turned back to what she was stirring on the stove. At the counter, Hildy, now wearing an apron, was peeling carrots.

"What's wrong with the water upstairs, Mrs. Hawkins?" Samantha asked. She glanced at two apple pies cooling on racks. The tempting smell made her realize how hungry she was.

"Oh, the well pump hasn't worked all day," Mrs. Hawkins replied. "There's no running water in the lodge at all. We've had to haul water from the lake in buckets." She pushed back wisps of white hair that straggled around her face. A smudge of flour dusted one cheek. Samantha was surprised to see Grandmary's always-in-control cook so flustered. Mrs. Hawkins handed Samantha a pitcher. "Would you mind helping out, dear, and get some ice for me?"

"Of course." Samantha took the pitcher and hurried toward the back door, where she picked up a lantern. Nellie followed.

"Where do we get ice?" Nellie asked.

"I'll show you. It's not delivered out here, the way it is in the city." Dusk was falling, and lanterns along the path glowed as Samantha led the way across the backyard toward a small, square wood-frame building. "In the winter, men cut blocks of ice from the lake and haul them up here on sleds. The icehouse keeps the ice frozen all summer." Samantha lifted the wooden bar that held the heavy icehouse door closed. A blast of cold air hit the girls as they stepped inside.

"I can hardly believe this," Nellie said, gazing around. "A whole room filled with ice. It's like a great big icebox."

"The walls are packed with sawdust to help keep the ice frozen. Those are meat storage boxes along the side." Samantha lifted the lantern higher so that Nellie could see.

On one wall hung two axes for chopping ice,

along with an ice saw, a big pair of ice tongs, and several ice picks. Samantha handed the pitcher to Nellie and grabbed a pick. She soon had the pitcher full of chunks of ice. "Let's get out of here," she said. "I'm freezing."

With a shiver, Nellie agreed. They hurried back outside, where it wasn't that much warmer.

"I'll show you around the grounds tomorrow," Samantha said as she replaced the bar across the icehouse door. "There are guest cabins on one side of the lodge, and the boathouse is down near the dock." Samantha pointed into the shadows to her right and added, "The cottage for the manager and his family is just past the icehouse."

"Jack and Homer," Nellie murmured. "They live so close."

"Maybe they won't be as much trouble as we think." Samantha tried to sound hopeful, but she felt worried. *They'd better not spoil our summer,* she thought.

Back in the kitchen, the girls stood close to Mrs. Hawkins's big stove, shivering until its heat made them warm again. Mrs. Hawkins had dinner ready. "Glenda, you can go now," she said. "Hildy and I will serve. Samantha, there's a pan of warm water here where you and Nellie can wash up."

The girls giggled as they splashed water and then dried their hands. But Samantha knew they had to put on proper faces before they went into the dining room. She took a deep breath and straightened her shoulders. Everyone else was already seated—Grandmary and the Admiral at the two ends of the long table, and Bridget, Jenny, and Trapper Jim along the sides. A fire danced in the fireplace, and candlelight made the china and silver gleam.

As soon as Samantha and Nellie took their places, Hildy ladled soup into bowls. Grandmary lifted her spoon, signaling that they could all begin. Samantha didn't have to be urged to eat. Lunch on the train had been a packed picnic from home, eaten hours ago. The only sounds for a few minutes were the clink of spoons on bowls and the crackling of the fire.

When she slowed her eating, Samantha took a good look at her grandmother. Grandmary looked tired and a little sad. Maybe the rainy weather had lowered her spirits.

"Are you happy with the new manager you hired, Grandmary?" Samantha asked.

Grandmary smiled. "The family seems to be working out well. Glenda is cheerful, and Mrs. Hawkins likes her. Mr. Griffith was wounded years ago in the Spanish-American War and walks with a limp, but he and the boys appear to be hard workers."

"I'm glad." Samantha hoped she had misjudged the boys. "I can't wait to go swimming when it stops raining," she continued. "Nellie knows how to swim, but we have to teach Bridget and Jenny. And I'm going to teach Nellie to canoe."

"Last week a huge tree fell across the back corner of the boathouse," the Admiral said. "The boats weren't damaged, but the tree had to be chopped up, and there were considerable repairs to the building. Both Burl Griffith and his boys were good help with that—weren't they, Jim?" the Admiral asked, bringing Jim into the conversation.

Jim enjoyed being invited for a meal at the lodge, but he was never very talkative. Maybe that was because he had spent so much time alone in the woods, Samantha thought. But she liked quiet people. She always wondered what they were thinking.

Jim nodded. "The Griffiths all seem to be hard workers. Mr. Griffith told me he's grateful for the job—he said most people wouldn't hire him because of his injury."

"I'm glad you gave him a chance, Grand-mary," Nellie said.

"It's a good thing he's here," the Admiral added. "There's been a lot of extra work this summer, what with the fallen tree and now the water not running. And there was a leak in our bedroom a few days ago, too. We found a hole in the roof where squirrels must have chewed their way in, hoping to find a dry nesting spot."

"Now that we're here, you can put us to

work," Nellie offered. She was used to working hard. Before she and her sisters had been adopted by Aunt Cornelia and Uncle Gard, she had worked in a factory and as a servant. When she first came to live with Samantha, it had been difficult for her to let someone else do the work she was used to doing.

"Thank you, Nellie, but no," Grandmary said. "This is your vacation. I want you to have a summer filled with fun."

"Maybe we *all* need to have some fun," Samantha said. "I have a wonderful idea! When we were boarding the ferry in the village, I noticed circus tents being set up. Maybe we should all go to the circus, Grandmary."

"A circus!" Bridget and Jenny said together, clapping their hands. "May we go, Grandmary? May we?" Bridget and Jenny were no longer the quiet, frightened little girls that Samantha had met nearly three years ago. Living with Aunt Cornelia and Uncle Gard, knowing they were safe, had made them blossom like spring flowers.

"We'll see," Grandmary said, but she was

smiling. That was a good sign.

"I haven't been to a circus in years," the Admiral said. He looked at Samantha with a twinkle in his blue eyes. He wanted to go, Samantha knew. He'd persuade Grandmary.

Samantha thought how glad she was that the Admiral was part of her family now. He and his first wife had lived in London, but they had been good friends with Grandmary and her husband, Samantha's grandfather. Together, the Admiral and his wife had often come to Piney Point to visit. Grandfather had died years ago. Then the Admiral's wife had died. Grandmary and the Admiral had kept visiting back and forth in London and New York, and the Admiral had kept coming to Piney Point in the summer.

Every year for the last few years, the Admiral had asked Grandmary to marry him. Finally she had said yes. Samantha thought it was a very romantic story. Grandmary seemed happier now, and the Admiral laughed all the time.

After dinner, Samantha and Nellie offered to help Mrs. Hawkins and Hildy clear the table and take dishes to the kitchen. But Mrs. Hawkins shooed them out. "Go and talk to your grandmother. She needs cheering up." Mrs. Hawkins put her finger over her lips. "But don't you dare tell her I said that."

"We won't," Samantha said. "Will we, Nellie?"

Nellie shook her head and followed Samantha back into the living room. Jim had just left. Grandmary and the Admiral were sitting in the rocking chairs by the fire. Bridget and Jenny sprawled on a big braided rug. They'd started a game of dominoes, but they were yawning.

"I think the rain has stopped," the Admiral said. "An almost-full moon has peeked through the clouds. I predict tomorrow will be warm and sunny. Why don't you girls go to bed so you'll be ready to have some fun?"

No one even thought of complaining. Bridget and Jenny jumped up and ran toward the stairs, leaving Samantha and Nellie to put away the dominoes. As soon as they finished, Nellie said good night and went upstairs, too. But Samantha lingered. Grandmary needed a hug tonight, and so did Samantha.

"I'm glad we're here, Grandmary," Samantha said, pressing her cheek against her grandmother's.

"I'm glad you're here, too. You'll bring the sunshine."

With a final good-night, Samantha left the room. But she hesitated on the bottom stair when she heard the Admiral ask Grandmary a question in a low tone. Samantha knew she shouldn't eavesdrop, but she sat in a shadow on the next-to-the-bottom stair and listened.

She heard Grandmary sigh. "Maybe we *should* sell the lodge, Archie," she said softly.

Sell the lodge? Samantha caught her breath and listened harder.

"There's so much maintenance, and there seems to be more every year," Grandmary went on. "Help is hard to get and keep, out here so far from the city. I'm surprised Cornelia was able to talk Hildy into coming. She's much younger than I expected."

"I thought so too, so I asked her. She's sixteen and small for her age." The Admiral paused, as if he was thinking about Grandmary's idea. "We've certainly had more than our share of problems this summer." The Admiral paused again, and Samantha knew he was taking a puff on his pipe. She could smell the sweet tobacco smoke from the stairway.

"I can't remember so many things going wrong or breaking down before," Grandmary said. "Of course, the lodge is getting old, and older places need more work. Mr. Diffenbacher has made a more-than-generous offer for Piney Point. Maybe it's time to sell, to stay in the city. Tell me what you think, Archie."

"I think you have to make that decision, Mary. But don't be hasty. Too much rain would discourage anyone, and goodness knows, we've had rain this summer. Why don't we wait for some sunny days? Big decisions should be made on sunny days."

"I'm sure you're right, but . . . I can't help but wonder if it's time."

THE CRY OF THE LOON

Samantha couldn't stand to hear any more. *Sell Piney Point? Grandmary loves Piney Point. I love Piney Point.* How could Grandmary even think of selling the lodge?

3
ENOUGH OF BOYS

Nellie shook Samantha awake the next morning. "Wake up, Samantha, wake up. The sun is shining."

Samantha sat up and rubbed her eyes, feeling groggy, as if she'd been caught in a bad dream. Then she realized that she *hadn't* been dreaming—she actually had overheard Grandmary and the Admiral talking about selling Piney Point. While she got dressed, she repeated every word of their conversation to Nellie.

"What can we do, Nellie? We have to change Grandmary's mind and keep her from selling."

Nellie hesitated. "It would be sad if she sold the lodge, Samantha, but I think the Admiral is right—it's up to your grandmother."

Samantha knew that, and yet she ached to

convince Grandmary that selling would be a
bad decision. Would Grandmary listen to her?
And, Samantha realized, if she said anything at
all, Grandmary would know that she had been
eavesdropping.

There was still no running water, so the girls
washed up with water set out in pitchers. Then
they hurried downstairs and into the kitchen.
Mrs. Hawkins was just lugging a bucket of water
to the sink.

"Good morning, Mrs. Hawkins," Samantha
said, pausing to sniff the delicious smell of a pan
of sweet rolls fresh from the oven.

"You and Nellie can sneak one." Mrs. Hawkins
set down the bucket and smiled.

Samantha took a warm roll and divided it
with Nellie. She savored a bite of the sweet
bread filled with cinnamon and raisins. Then
she turned back to the cook. "Do you like
coming to Piney Point every summer, Mrs.
Hawkins?" she asked.

The cook gave her a puzzled glance. "Of
course, Samantha. We escape the heat of town,

the noise and the dirt. Piney Point is a special place. Why do you ask?"

"Oh, I was just wondering." It didn't seem as if Mrs. Hawkins had heard anything about Grandmary selling the lodge. "We'll be back in a few minutes. I want to show Nellie around."

"You can go tell Mrs. Griffith that with Hildy here, I won't need her until noon."

"All right." Samantha took Nellie's hand and headed outside. She took a deep breath. The morning smelled fresh and clean. Beams of sunshine sparkled through the pines. A robin warbled, surely singing about the glorious day. "Oh, Nellie, could the woods be any more beautiful? I do love it here, don't you?"

Nellie laughed. "Give me a few days to get used to the quiet. I miss the hustle and bustle of the city."

Samantha led the way down the well-worn path they'd taken last night to a log cottage that faced the thick pinewoods. A small garden was green with lacy rows of lettuce and spinach. The cottage's window boxes spilled out pink and white petunias. Samantha knocked on the door.

Glenda Griffith came to the screen, wiping her hands on her apron. "Hello, girls. You're up early. Would you like to come in?" Mrs. Griffith held open the door.

"Just for a minute." Samantha was too curious to say no. "We came to tell you that Mrs. Hawkins doesn't need you until noon."

The small house was full of color. Dark brown furniture crowded the living room, with several patchwork pillows on each piece. Slightly faded blue curtains hung at the windows, but a patchwork border made them look nearly new. A knitted throw of brown, orange, and gold was draped across the sofa. Samantha could see into only one bedroom. The bed was covered with a pieced quilt.

"Did you make the lovely quilt, Mrs. Griffith?" Samantha asked.

"Yes. I can't sit still even when the house-work is done. I like to keep my hands busy."

"Grandmary, the Admiral, and Jim say all your family is hardworking," Nellie said.

Mrs. Griffith smiled. "I'm so glad that your grandmother hired us. It's so quiet and peaceful here. My husband and I never liked the city."

"We'd better go, Mrs. Griffith. I want to show Nellie around before breakfast," Samantha said, stepping outside. She led Nellie farther along the path. "Let's go the long way around. I'll show you the guest cottages." Samantha pointed to a distant spit of land along the lake-shore and added, "Grandmary's property goes way down there, to a small fishing and hunting camp on the lake. Then it runs up the mountain behind us. We'll go hiking up the mountain in a few days."

They came up around the front of two small but inviting log cottages. Wicker chairs sat on both porches. "These are for guests. And see that tiny cabin back over there? Grandmary told Trapper Jim last summer that he could stay there any time."

"I can see that he's a good friend." Nellie hurried to keep up with Samantha as she ran down the hill to the lake.

Sunshine sparkled off the surface of the water like a net made of thousands of diamonds. Just as the girls stopped at the shoreline, a fish jumped high into the air.

Samantha laughed. "The sunshine makes me feel the same way. Like jumping up and down, or going swimming, or—or just running." She took off along the sandy shore toward the dock, Nellie at her heels. "Look at all the new shingles on the boathouse. That must have been a mess to clean up."

As the girls stared at the boathouse roof, a single loon sailed by the dock toward a stand of pines that came all the way down to the lake. The loon's black back, spotted with white, gleamed in the sun. "Do you think its nest is down there?" Nellie whispered.

"It's just on the other side of the trees, I think," Samantha whispered back. She started up the hill to the lodge.

They were near the laundry shed when Samantha and Nellie heard a soft thud, and then another. The girls stopped, listening. Samantha looked up into the tree branches, expecting to see a squirrel dropping acorns. Instead, she caught sight of Jack and Homer up ahead, leaning against two pine trees, tossing cones at the shed.

"It's so boring here," Jack was saying. "In another year or two, we can go off on our own, back to New York City or anywhere else we want. We could even go out West and be cowboys."

Samantha rolled her eyes at Nellie, who stifled a giggle.

"Too bad Pa likes it here so much," Homer said. "If Mrs. Beemis would hurry up and sell this place, we might get out of here sooner."

How did Jack and Homer know about the possibility of Grandmary's selling? Suddenly Samantha had heard enough. She marched over to the boys, with Nellie close behind her. "My grandmother is not selling!" Instantly she felt embarrassed at her outburst. She wasn't sure *what* Grandmary was going to do.

Jack and Homer looked up in surprise. Then Homer grinned. "Hey, you girls. Did you get over being scared of a bird?" He pursed his lips and imitated the loon call again.

"Your silly joke didn't scare us," Samantha said. She grabbed Nellie's hand, and they pushed past the two boys.

But the boys followed. "What do you do here all day?" Homer asked. "It's too quiet. Unless we've got work to do, I'm bored."

"How can you be bored?" Samantha replied. "You can hike, fish, swim—"

Jack laughed. "Do you girls even know how to swim?"

"Bet you can't paddle a canoe," Homer added with a grin.

"Bet I can. Excuse me, we have to go now." Samantha was relieved to hear Mrs. Griffith call Jack and Homer. It seemed as though the boys were always going to be underfoot.

Before the girls reached the lodge, they heard the Admiral talking and headed in the direction of his voice. They found him in the pump house with a man Samantha didn't know. Both men were leaning over some equipment, their heads bent. All Samantha could see of the second man was his curly, steel-gray hair.

"Have you figured out why the water's not running?" Samantha asked the Admiral.

"Yes," he replied. "There's dirt in the pump engine." He took off his hat and scratched his head, thinking.

"How would dirt get into the pump?" Nellie asked.

"That's what we're trying to figure out. Nellie and Samantha, this is Burl Griffith. He's our new manager."

The two men stood. Mr. Griffith was shorter than the Admiral, but his arms bulged with muscles. Samantha resisted looking at his legs, remembering that one had been injured in the war. His eyes were brown and his face weathered. He reminded Samantha of Geppetto, the man in one of Jenny's favorite tales. Geppetto was a wood-carver who wanted a son so badly, he carved a puppet that he named Pinocchio and pretended he was real. But Mr. Griffith certainly didn't have to wish he had a son.

"Pleased to meet you, Mr. Griffith," Samantha and Nellie said together, remembering their manners.

Mr. Griffith returned to studying the pump parts. "I reckon all the rain has washed dirt into the system," he said to the Admiral. "Far as I can figure, if we clean this up, oil it, and put it back together, it should work fine."

"Mrs. Hawkins will be glad," Samantha said. She and Nellie hurried to go tell her.

When they got back to the kitchen, Mrs. Hawkins was sliding a second pan of sweet rolls from the oven. Hildy stood at the kitchen table, whipping a bowl of eggs into a froth.

Mrs. Hawkins was delighted that the pump would be repaired soon. "That's good news. And the sun is out, too. Maybe our bad luck is turning around." Mrs. Hawkins poured the eggs into a skillet. "Go on into the dining room, girls. We'll be right in with sausage and eggs."

The girls found Bridget and Jenny already seated at the dining table with Grandmary. Jenny set down her glass of milk and asked eagerly, "Are we going to the circus today, Samantha?"

The circus—Samantha had almost forgotten! She glanced at Grandmary, who smiled.

"It's up to the Admiral," Grandmary said, placing a sweet roll on her plate and passing the dish to Nellie.

"Did I hear someone speak my name?" The Admiral stopped to kiss Grandmary on the cheek before he sat down. His blue eyes twinkled and teased the girls. Samantha couldn't imagine his not being part of their family. And Grandmary brightened the minute he walked into the room.

"Please, please, Admiral," Bridget pleaded. "May we go to the circus?"

Jenny clapped her hands since her mouth was too full to speak.

"Yes, yes, yes," Grandmary said with a laugh. "Take these noisy children somewhere, Archie."

"Piney Point has been too quiet, though, don't you think, Mary?" His eyes softened as he looked at Grandmary. "Don't you want to go to the circus, too?"

Grandmary smiled at the Admiral. "If you don't mind, Archie, I think I'll stay behind and relax. I'm going to sit in my rocker on the porch, listen for the loons, and enjoy the sunshine."

Samantha wished her grandmother would go, but when Grandmary made a decision, there was no talking her out of it.

"All right. Does anyone else want to stay behind?" The Admiral looked around as if any of the girls were going to choose not to go. Bridget held her hand over her mouth to keep a giggle in. Jenny shook her head, her eyes huge and sparkling with delight.

Samantha felt terribly excited herself.

4
ANOTHER ACCIDENT

"See how much prettier the lake looks in the sunshine?" Samantha said to her sisters as they boarded the ferryboat to go to the village. "And look, fish are jumping way out there in the middle."

"I see one!" Jenny squealed. "I'm going to count them."

While Nellie, Bridget, and Jenny leaned over the boat railing and looked at the sparkling water and the waves dancing behind them, Samantha stayed close to the Admiral. "Grandmary looks tired, Admiral. Is she all right? I'd think she'd be excited about her birthday."

"Young people are excited about birthdays, Samantha. But your grandmother is worried about everything that's happened lately. Having to find a new manager on short notice wasn't easy, either."

"What can I do?"

"Give her lots of attention and hugs, whether or not she seems to want them. You could cheer up a tree stump, Samantha."

Samantha laughed, tried to put her own worrying aside, and walked over to join Nellie. The Admiral stood behind them.

What a difference the sunshine made. The ferryboat passed stands of deep woods where huge pines mixed with balsam and spruce trees. A deer and her fawn stood at the shoreline, drinking from the lake. The mother looked up, but she seemed accustomed to boats going by and didn't move. As the miles passed, Samantha enjoyed watching Nellie and the girls, who were amazed at seeing so much land with no people.

"Look, Admiral, I never saw those before." Samantha pointed toward two new cottages on the lakeshore. "When were they built?"

"This spring, as soon as the snow started

melting, I assume. Jim told me that someone had sold a big piece of land here. The buyer divided it into five- or six-acre lots and sold them to city folks. There are probably more houses being built that we can't see."

"I guess more and more people from the city want to get away for the summer. But they're bringing the city here, don't you think?"

"I do indeed. I come out here to get away from people." The Admiral filled his pipe and lit it.

"If Grandmary sells Piney Point, will it be divided up into little pieces?"

The Admiral looked at Samantha. She realized she wasn't supposed to know about that. She didn't confess how she found out. "I don't know," he said quietly. "Maybe."

"I don't want her to sell Piney Point. Do you, Admiral?"

The Admiral didn't answer immediately. "No, Samantha, I don't," he said finally. "But it's not our decision. And promise me you won't worry her about this, or even tell her that you know about the possibility."

"I promise, Admiral," Samantha said reluctantly.

They got off the boat at the village dock in time to see a band dressed in blue and gold uniforms playing marching music. Bridget and Jenny held hands and started to march along the crowded street toward huge white tents in a field. Calliope music floated on the breeze, and Samantha saw a Ferris wheel turning above the tents.

"Stay right with us, girls," Nellie called. "You could get lost in the crowd." She hurried to keep up with them.

"Samantha, I have a lot of change here," the Admiral said, digging into his pocket. "Take this for some rides and whatever else you girls want. If you'll stay together, I won't try to keep up. I have several things to do. I'll find you when it's time to start back to Piney Point."

Samantha took the coins and nodded. *Maybe the Admiral has some special shopping to do for Grandmary,* she thought as she went off to join her sisters. It gave her an idea. She and Nellie had brought handkerchiefs they'd embroidered for Grandmary's birthday gift, but maybe they could find something extra for her today, too.

"Let's ride the Ferris wheel, Samantha," Bridget called. She and Jenny rushed up to Samantha and Nellie, grabbed their hands, and tugged them toward the big wheel slowly turning round, carrying people in chairs that tilted back and forth if the passengers didn't sit still. Samantha knew Bridget and Jenny would never sit still.

"All right, Jenny. The Admiral gave us some spending money. You ride with me. Bridget can ride with Nellie." Samantha walked up to the booth and bought four tickets.

As they waited in line, Samantha looked around. She would have preferred to stroll the fairgrounds first, to see everything there was to do. She caught a brief glimpse of the Admiral making his way through the crowds.

The wheel stopped and let off passengers. Their turn had finally come. Nellie and Bridget got into a chair, and then the wheel went up a little, letting Samantha and Jenny get into the next chair. Up and up they slowly climbed until all the chairs were full. Then the wheel turned faster, but not so fast as to be scary.

Maybe this ride was a good idea after all, Samantha thought. As they reached the top of the Ferris wheel, she could see the entire circus laid out below them. A field of tents bloomed like huge white blossoms. A walkway lined with booths ran down the middle. Games, food, side-shows—what should they do and see next?

"Stop leaning forward and wiggling around so much, Samantha," Jenny said. "It's scary when the chair rocks back and forth."

Samantha smiled. She had thought Jenny would be the one rocking the chair. "Have you been on a Ferris wheel before, Jenny?"

"No, but I saw a picture once." Jenny held on tightly to the wooden bar that kept them in the seat, her knuckles white. "It's kind of fun."

By the time the ride ended, Jenny had started rocking the chair herself. "Look down there,

44

Samantha. How tiny those horses look from up here! They're doing tricks. Can we go watch them?"

After they got off the Ferris wheel, it was obvious who was going to be in charge. Samantha and Nellie laughed as they ran after the younger girls, making sure they didn't lose sight of them.

"Next is the merry-go-round." Bridget stopped and got in line. "I want a black horse. Jenny, you get white—that's my second favorite."

"I'll pay for this ride, Samantha," Nellie said. "I earned extra money at school tutoring younger children." She hurried away to the ticket booth.

As soon as Samantha climbed onto her horse, she spotted the Admiral again. She waved, but he was busy talking to a man she didn't recognize. The man had a big handlebar mustache and reddish hair. He was showing the Admiral something in a large pasteboard folder. The Admiral nodded, pulled out his wallet and gave the man money, then clapped him on the back. The calli-ope music started and the horses went round. By the time the merry-go-round had made its first circle, the Admiral was gone.

When the ride ended, Samantha was still wondering what the men had been looking at. Nellie interrupted her thoughts. "I want to buy Grandmary a present before I run out of money," Nellie said. She took Bridget's hand on one side and Jenny's on the other. "Do not dash away again," she ordered in a stern voice.

The girls stopped at a booth where a young woman was handing out free samples of deli-cious maple sugar candy. Nellie examined the boxes that were displayed for sale. "Look how the sugar was poured into a mold so that there's a design on the top," she said.

"I made those candies myself after we tapped our trees this spring," the young woman replied. "A box makes a nice gift."

"Grandmary likes sweets," Samantha said, encouraging Nellie. After Nellie made her pur-chase, the girls continued down the row of booths.

They stopped by a woman dancing in a costume that looked like a hundred scarves sewn together. The skirt swirled out so that all the colors mixed like a dancing rainbow.

"Would you like to buy a pretty scarf?" an older woman seated at a booth asked Samantha. "Made of silk, brought all the way from India."

Samantha knew that Grandmary would love a scarf. She picked up one in a perfect shade of blue, but the woman named a price that was too high. Before Samantha could respond, Nellie started to bargain. Samantha listened, then hid a smile as the woman agreed on a price that Samantha could afford.

"I learned to do that in the market when our family had so little money," Nellie whispered as they left the booth. Then her smile faded. "Now where are Bridget and Jenny? They can disappear faster than a magician's rabbit."

They found the girls watching two jugglers tossing balls and small bowling pins back and forth. Then the girls wandered together, taking in the sights. They saw a tiger pacing in its cage, a lion whose roar made Bridget and Jenny jump back and gasp, and a contortionist folding himself into a small box.

Samantha and Nellie bought warm buns filled with spicy sausages, and the four girls nibbled them as they walked. Further on, a small cinnamon-colored bear charmed them. When its trainer played a harmonica, the bear stood up on its hind legs and danced. Round and round the bear turned. Bridget and Jenny squealed with delight and didn't want to leave.

In addition to watching the bear, Samantha amused herself by watching the crowd. To her right, she caught sight of the Admiral's red-haired friend standing beside a tall, handsome man. The tall man pulled a light brown paper from a satchel. He did all the talking while the Admiral's friend studied the paper and nodded. Finally the tall man smiled, handed the paper over, shook hands, and left quickly.

Just as the bear stopped dancing, Samantha heard the Admiral's voice behind her. "Are you girls ready to go home? We need to get back before dark—and of course we don't want to miss dinner."

With a last look back at the circus, wishing they could stay for the evening's acts in the tents, they walked back to the dock where the ferry captain had said he'd pick them up and take them back to Piney Point.

"Who was that man you were talking to, Admiral?" Samantha asked while they waited for the boat. "The one with the reddish hair?"

"Let me think. I talked to so many people today."

"He had a big handlebar mustache," Samantha prompted. She was sure the Admiral wouldn't have forgotten him.

But the Admiral only shrugged and turned to the other girls. "Did you have fun?" he asked them.

"Oh, yes!" Nellie, Jenny, and Bridget said together. Bridget added, "When we tell Grandmary about the dancing bear and the rides, she'll wish she had come with us."

On the boat, they sat on a bench out of the wind. The other girls told the Admiral all about their day at the circus, but Samantha was quiet. The circus had been wonderful, but why had the Admiral pretended not to know who Samantha was asking about? It seemed almost as if he was hiding something. Did it have something to do with Grandmary's birthday?

Finally the ferryboat let them off at Piney Point, and they started up the path toward the lodge. Trapper Jim met them halfway. "Admiral, hurry along," he said quietly. "Mrs. Beemis has had an accident."

Samantha's heart lurched. She took off running with the Admiral and Jim.

5

SUSPICION WITHOUT PROOF

When the Admiral, Jim, and the girls reached the lodge, Grandmary was in the living room lying on the sofa, her ankle wrapped and propped on a pillow. Hildy sat on a stool nearby. "Grandmary, are you all right?" Samantha asked, hurrying to her grandmother's side.

"Oh, yes, I was just clumsy. I thought it was time for the ferry to return, so I decided to walk down to the dock and wait for you."

"She fell on the porch steps, Admiral Beemis," Hildy explained. "I did what I could to help her."

"You did a good job, Hildy," Grandmary said. "Thank you."

Hildy left as the Admiral pulled a rocking chair close to Grandmary and took her hand.

"Tell us exactly what happened. Are you sure you're all right, Mary?"

"Now, don't make a fuss. I didn't fall far. I had nearly reached the bottom step. I—I think perhaps a step broke."

"Broke! How could that happen?" the Admiral said. "I made sure this house was ship-shape when we arrived this summer. I thought I checked the porch steps."

Hildy returned, carrying a heavy tray filled with a teapot, cups and saucers, and a plate of sugar cookies. She set the tray on a low table near the sofa. "Mrs. Hawkins says a nice cup of tea will make everyone feel better." She lifted the pot and poured the first serving into an eggshell-thin cup painted with roses.

Grandmary, with the Admiral's help, sat up straighter and took the cup and saucer. "Look at all of you, sitting in a line like birds on a tree limb. Shoo, go into the dining room and have your tea in a proper manner. Then I suggest you girls rest before dinner. I know you've had a big day."

Reluctantly, Samantha followed her sisters and Hildy to the dining-room table. Samantha accepted a cup of tea from Hildy and sipped it, staring at the tablecloth. She nibbled a cookie, but crumbs caught in her throat as she tried to swallow.

We shouldn't have left Grandmary alone, she thought. There had been park benches all around the fairgrounds. Grandmary could have sat down when she was tired and watched the crowds of people and performers go by. Samantha had never thought about Grandmary getting old, but, looking at her on the sofa, Samantha noticed that Grandmary's soft gray eyes were tired, and tiny lines ran down her pale cheeks.

Grandmary would never use the word *old*, and she had never before seemed old to Samantha. Of course, Samantha had never seen Grandmary helpless and hurt before, either.

Slowly, Samantha and her sisters climbed the stairs to their rooms. The joy had gone out of the day. Bridget and Jenny fell asleep the minute that

Samantha and Nellie pulled a blanket over them, but Samantha and Nellie couldn't sleep.

"We should have insisted that Grandmary go with us to the circus, Nellie," Samantha said as she paced the floor of their room. "She would have gone if we'd begged her to."

"She wanted to stay here, Samantha. The accident didn't happen because she stayed here without us. She could have fallen any time, with us here or not."

Samantha knew that Nellie was right, but she couldn't stop her thoughts from churning. She flopped on her bed, her mind a clutter of worries and ideas. She would have preferred to relive the fun of the circus, but those memories had been pushed aside by Grandmary's accident.

Grandmary's accident. Had it really been an accident? Of course it was, Samantha told herself. How could she think otherwise? Samantha glanced at the other bed and saw that Nellie was wide-awake.

"Nellie, don't you think there've been a lot of accidents here this summer?" Samantha asked.

"A tree fell on the boathouse. Something made a hole in the roof. Dirt got into the well pump." She paused. "The pump is protected inside the well house, so how could dirt have gotten into the pump engine?"

"I wondered about that too," Nellie said, "but maybe there was a bad windstorm the night the tree fell. The storm could have blown dirt through cracks into the pump house, too." Nellie shrugged. "Or it could all be just a run of bad luck. My mama always said bad luck comes in threes." Nellie turned and looked at Samantha, a frown on her face. "You don't really think someone is *making* things go wrong, do you?"

Samantha thought for a minute. "Homer and Jack seem to want to leave Piney Point. Do you think *they'd* cause accidents, hoping their pa would get fired or quit?"

"That would be a pretty rotten thing to do." Nellie sat up. "I want to see the broken step."

"Good idea. Maybe we can figure out why it broke. The Admiral checked those steps less than a month ago, and I know he wouldn't have

missed seeing that a step was weak or cracked."
Samantha tugged on her shoes and quickly laced
them.

Nellie jumped up, put her shoes on, and
grabbed a sweater against the evening's chill.

The girls heard Grandmary and the Admiral
talking in the living room, so they went to the
kitchen and tiptoed quietly past Mrs. Hawkins,
who was lifting something that smelled rich and
delicious from the oven. They slipped out the
back door. No one was outside.

The sun was sinking below the trees, making shadows long and light dim. Samantha led
the way, staying off the path and keeping to the
shadows thrown by the house. A couple of times
she slid on pine needles, but she kept her balance
and hurried on.

The dusk was quiet, much too quiet. No
loon called, no owl hooted, no breeze swished
through the pine trees.

As they neared the front of the lodge, they
heard voices. Carefully they looked around the
corner. Three people were hunched over the

steps. Samantha and Nellie exchanged glances. It was Mr. Griffith and his sons. Homer was holding a lantern for his father to work by. "You got it, Pa," he said. "It's perfect now. No one can even tell the step was broken."

"Yeah," Jack agreed. He held a long, flat piece of wood in both hands.

Samantha took a deep breath and walked toward them, Nellie right behind her. "What are you doing?" Samantha asked, speaking more loudly than she meant to.

Homer spun around. He looked surprised to see Samantha and Nellie. "Fixing the step," he replied. "What do you think?"

"Why didn't you wait until tomorrow, when the light would be better?" Nellie asked.

"We didn't want someone else to fall," Burl Griffith said simply. Jack helped his father to his feet, and he gathered his tools. "Come on, boys. Must be suppertime."

The Griffiths left, Homer holding the lantern and Jack carrying the long piece of wood. Samantha felt slightly foolish, and frustrated too.

If anyone *had* caused Grandmary's accident, the evidence was gone now.

"Do you think it's odd that they were in such a hurry to fix the step?" she whispered to Nellie.

Nellie shook her head. "It's what a good manager *would* do," she said quietly. After a moment, she added, "Of course, if Jack and Homer did anything to damage that step, Mr. Griffith probably wouldn't have been able to tell in the darkness."

A loon chose that moment to call with its wavering voice: *Ooo-oooo. Ooo-oooo. Ooo–oooo.*

"I'll never get used to that sound," Nellie said, shivering. "Let's go see if dinner's ready."

Carefully, they tested the new board, then ran up the rest of the porch steps. The door creaked as they entered the living room. "There you are," Hildy said. "Mrs. Beemis sent me to find you. Was the circus wonderful?" There was a note of sadness in Hildy's voice that Samantha couldn't ignore.

"Yes," she replied. "I'm really sorry you

couldn't come with us, Hildy. But I'm glad you were here to help Grandmary."

The Admiral, Grandmary, Jim, and the younger girls were seated at the dining table. Quickly, Samantha and Nellie joined them. Samantha couldn't stop thinking about the broken step.

After Hildy had served her, Samantha took a few bites of Mrs. Hawkins's delicious baked trout. Then she cleared her throat. "Grandmary, when you fell, who heard you? Who came to help you?"

"Oh, do we have to go over that story again, Samantha? I'd like to forget all about it. I'm not badly hurt. I'll be walking around as good as new in a few days."

Hildy took the dish of potatoes she had passed and placed it on a sideboard. "I heard Mrs. Beemis cry out. I realized I couldn't lift her, so I called for help. Mr. Griffith came, both his boys, Glenda, Mrs. Hawkins, and even Jim, who was cleaning fish for dinner."

Grandmary frowned at Hildy, who quickly

got busy fetching another dish of food. But Grandmary finished the story. "I was so embarrassed. I've never been clumsy before."

And were you clumsy today? Samantha had her doubts, but she had no way to prove her suspicions. Then she thought of the long piece of wood Jack had been carrying a few minutes ago. It had to have been the broken step. Just maybe, she thought, she still had a chance to see it.

After dinner Bridget and Jenny went upstairs. The household quickly became quiet. Samantha put her finger over her lips and motioned to Nellie. Telling no one of her plans, she and Nellie slipped past Mrs. Hawkins and Hildy as they washed dishes, took a pocket torch from beside the back door, and stepped outside. Easing the door shut behind them, they listened but heard no sounds except the faint murmurs of night.

"Where are we going?" Nellie whispered.

"*Shhh.* Just follow me." Samantha's feet knew

every inch of Piney Point's paths, and the moon was almost full. She didn't need the pocket torch yet. She hurried toward the shed where the manager's tools and supplies were stored.

The shed door creaked as Samantha opened it. She waited to see if anyone had heard. Then she and Nellie stepped inside.

Samantha snapped on the pocket torch. She remembered that their former manager, Mr. Shoemaker, had kept scrap wood in a stack beside the counter piled with tools. The stack of scrap was still there. She searched among fence posts, some old window frames, and boards. The piece of wood from the broken step was tucked at the back of the stack. She reached, pulled it out, and laid it on the counter, focusing the flashlight beam on the broken end.

"Look at that, Nellie," she whispered.

The top was splintered where it had given way, but the underside had been neatly cut. Samantha fingered the fresh saw marks. The cuts smelled of cedar sawdust.

"Do you think someone made those cuts

before the step broke, to weaken it?" Nellie's voice wobbled at the shock of their discovery.

"That must be what happened."

"What should we do? Should we take the board inside?"

Samantha hesitated, thinking. Then she put the board back exactly where she'd found it. "No. In the morning, I'll bring the Admiral here to see this for himself. He'll know what to do next."

Without a sound, Samantha snapped off her light. She and Nellie slipped out of the shed and tiptoed back to the lodge.

6
THE STRANGER
ON THE MOUNTAIN

The next morning at breakfast, sunlight streamed through the windows, but everyone seemed to share Samantha and Nellie's quiet mood.

As the family was finishing breakfast, Grandmary said firmly, "I want everyone to stop worrying about me. Samantha, I know how much you like hiking and exploring when you're at Piney Point. Go ask Mrs. Hawkins to make you some picnic lunches. You and the girls ought to enjoy the outdoors while the sun is shining. Take your sketchbooks. Draw me some pictures, since I won't be able to go for a walk anytime soon."

"I will, Grandmary. It's a perfect day for a hike," Samantha said. "Nellie, will you take charge of getting us organized? I need to speak to the Admiral." Nellie would know why that was so important.

"All right. We'll meet you at the back door in a few minutes."

Samantha spotted the Admiral outside by the pump house and hurried to him. "Admiral, are you busy? I need to show you something."

The Admiral looked surprised to see Samantha. "I just checked the pump. It seems to be working fine." He smiled down at her. "Now, what do you *need* to show me?"

Samantha glanced around and then led the Admiral to the storage shed. She motioned him inside, a finger to her lips. She went straight to the stack of scrap wood, explaining quietly, "Last night, after Mr. Griffith fixed the stairs, I—" She stopped short, feeling sick. The broken step was gone!

As she turned back to the Admiral, she saw Glenda Griffith poking her head through the door. "Is there a problem, Admiral Beemis?" she asked.

Samantha's heart pounded, but the Admiral seemed perfectly calm. "Oh, good morning, Glenda," he said. "I believe Samantha was just going to show me something. Perhaps she wanted to see more of Jack's work. The moose he carved for Bridget and Jenny was grand." Mrs. Griffith looked pleased at the Admiral's words.

He moved to a shelf that ran the length of one wall. "Look over here, Samantha." Samantha and Mrs. Griffith followed him.

Samantha felt her eyes grow wide, then wider. She took a deep breath. On the shelf was a lifelike wooden loon, and an owl so beautifully detailed that it looked ready to hoot and fly away.

"Jack—Jack made these?" Samantha stuttered.

"Jack is a real artist, Samantha," the Admiral said. "He has a special talent."

Samantha was so surprised that she almost forgot the broken step. Reaching out, she dared to touch the loon. Its smooth, shiny surface had been polished to a lovely black sheen.

"Thank you, Admiral and Mrs. Griffith, for

sharing Jack's work." Samantha swallowed hard. "But I have to go. Nellie and the girls are waiting for me."

Samantha turned and escaped the closeness of the small workshop. Had she let her imagination run away with her last night? Maybe Jack had simply taken the porch step to use for carving. And maybe the saw marks—well, Mr. Griffith would have had to saw off the broken step before putting in a new one. *I don't know anything about carpentry or repairing stairs*, she admitted to herself. *Maybe I just believed what I wanted to believe—that someone tried to cause an accident.*

A peal of laughter interrupted her thoughts. She had nearly reached the laundry shed, and she saw that Hildy was talking with Jack and Homer there.

"Good morning, Samantha," Hildy said, her face flushed. Jack and Homer grinned and returned to hauling wood for the laundry fire that crackled under a big black cast-iron pot. Hildy poured a bucket of water into a rinsing tub, then stepped around a pile of dirty sheets. "I've never done laundry outside before," she told Samantha as she added a stick of wood to the fire.

The fire flickered higher. Suddenly Samantha gasped, and her hand flew to her mouth. Under the wash pot, already being consumed in the flames, was the broken step. A corner of the board still stuck out of the fire, so Samantha recognized it clearly. But she was too late to pull the board from the fire. Samantha watched flames lick along the board and curl around the very end.

"Is something wrong, Samantha?" Hildy asked.

Before Samantha could find an answer, Glenda Griffith joined them. "What's taking so long, Hildy? I thought you'd have the sheets washed and rinsed by now." She turned to Jack and Homer, who had walked up with another load of firewood. "That's enough wood. You boys get out of here. Find your father. He'll have plenty of work for you to do."

"Yes, ma'am," Jack said. He winked at Hildy before sauntering away, whistling a cheery tune.

Samantha watched the boys leave, then watched the last of the porch step crumble into ashes, any evidence of wrongdoing gone.

Samantha, Nellie, and the younger girls set off on their hike a few minutes later, their pack baskets full of sandwiches, sketchbooks, and pencils. Bridget and Jenny, chattering with excitement, ran ahead, taking little side trips into the woods to explore. The day sparkled, with not a cloud in sight. A flock of geese, moving from one lake to another, seemed to swim across the sky. Birds called from high in the pines. Squirrels scolded the girls for disturbing them without bringing food to share.

"What happened, Samantha?" Nellie asked softly. "I can tell you're upset. What did the Admiral say about the step?"

"Oh, Nellie, the step is gone, burned up in the fire under the wash pot." She told Nellie the whole story. "I should have brought the step back into the lodge last night. If the Admiral could only have seen it, he might have been able to tell whether it was damaged on purpose."

"You couldn't have known the step would be gone this morning," Nellie said loyally. "But doesn't it seem suspicious that the board was used as firewood so quickly? Maybe— maybe someone saw us go into the shed last night and wanted to be sure that nobody else could take a look at those saw marks."

Samantha shivered at that idea.

"Just tell the Admiral what you saw last night," Nellie urged her. "I'll tell him I saw the marks, too."

Samantha glanced at Nellie. "He'll probably say that our imaginations are running away with us. And—and maybe that's true. Maybe all the accidents and my worries about Grand-mary selling the lodge are making us jump to conclusions." Samantha sighed. "I don't think we have enough proof to talk to the Admiral yet. But it makes me really angry to think that those two boys could be causing such trouble just because they don't want to live here. I think we have to keep an eye on Jack and Homer as much as possible."

Nellie gave a determined nod. "They don't know that we suspect them, so they'll slip up soon." She shifted her pack basket to her other shoulder.

After some hard uphill climbing, Samantha had walked off her anger and disappointment. She pointed to an outcropping of huge rocks, some smooth and flat, almost like seats waiting for someone to sit and soak up the sun. "There it is—over there," she said. "My favorite spot to have a picnic."

The girls spread their picnic blanket on the ground, then opened the baskets to see what Mrs. Hawkins had packed.

After lunch, Bridget and Jenny gathered pinecones, stuck twigs in them for arms and legs, and made the creatures talk. As Samantha watched, she remembered the beautiful carved loon Jack had made, and she had a wonderful idea. Could the girls make pinecone loons to decorate the table for Grandmary's birthday party? Their loons wouldn't look as perfect as Jack's, but she knew that Grandmary would like them.

Then her stomach twisted at an awful thought: *Will this be Grandmary's last birthday at Piney Point?*

She lay back and took deep breaths, studying some fast-moving clouds that had drifted in. She willed herself to stop thinking worrisome thoughts and enjoy the perfect day. Then she took out her sketchbook. Grandmary wanted some pictures from their hike. Samantha decided that she'd try to capture their picnic rocks, the huge pines around them, and a few clouds in a sky that was the exact shade of blue that Grandmary loved.

"We don't want to draw now, Samantha," Bridget said.

"Then you and Jenny collect a lot of these pinecones for an art project I've thought of. You can fill our baskets now that the lunch is gone."

The younger girls set off happily, and Samantha and Nellie began to sketch. Samantha struggled with her drawing. Her rocks looked like big gray blobs, and her clouds resembled floating cauliflower. She started over twice, then sighed. "I am not an artist. Let me see your drawing, Nellie."

Nellie held out her sketchbook and glanced around. "Where are Bridget and Jenny?"

Samantha looked across the rocky clearing. "I don't see them. Maybe they went farther into the woods looking for pinecones." She stood up and called, "Bridget! Jenny! Where are you?" No small voices answered. No little girls came running. "You go that way, Nellie," said Samantha. "I'll look over here."

Samantha hurried into the woods, but there was no path, and soon the underbrush was so thick that she could go no further.

Nellie came running from the other side of the path. "I don't see them anywhere."

Samantha started packing up her supplies.

"Do you think they went back to the lodge?"

"Surely not. And would they know the way?" Nellie grabbed her pack basket and stuffed her sketchbook and pencils inside.

"Stay calm. They can't have gone far. Look, here are our footprints coming up the mountain. And none go down."

Nellie caught on quickly. "Here, Samantha, look." She pointed at two different prints of small shoes going uphill from the rocks and into the thick pine forest. "I think they went on up the mountain without us."

"Oh, dear. Hurry, let's follow them. There's hardly any trail, but look—someone slid in the pine needles here," Samantha said. She and Nellie were soon breathing hard, but they kept climbing.

The footprints disappeared, but here and there, the forest floor looked disturbed. They found an area in the forest where brush didn't grow as thick, as if there had been a trail once. A broken limb gave them another clue, and then Nellie grabbed Jenny's hair ribbon, dangling from a low limb like a flag.

"What were they thinking, running off like this?" Nellie asked, catching her breath.

"They weren't thinking. And they must have been running. We've come farther in this direction than I've ever been from the lodge."

"Brid-get! Jen-ny!" Nellie called. No one answered. Nellie and Samantha exchanged anxious glances.

"The sun's still high," Samantha assured Nellie. "I'm not going to worry yet."

Way at the top of the ridge, beyond the shadowy trees, Samantha and Nellie came out into a beautiful meadow full of wildflowers of every color. Mountains, smoky blue, rose up in the distance. This seemed to be another world— a magical world.

Across the clearing, Samantha spotted Bridget, sitting cross-legged in the grass. Nearby, a man stood before an easel, painting. As Samantha ran closer, she saw that Bridget was painting, too. A short distance away, Jenny sat in the grass, using colored pencils to draw a cluster of blue and yellow and white blossoms.

"Bridget and Jenny," Nellie scolded. "Have you any idea how frightened I was? What made you think it was all right to run off and leave us?"

"I'm sorry, Nellie," Bridget said. "But isn't it pretty up here? And this nice man is a painter. He's letting us paint too." Bridget had washed the bottom of her paper with green, then dappled a rainbow of colors on top to suggest the wildflowers. The green was topped by dark blue mountains and the lighter blue sky. Samantha had to admit that the picture was lovely. She didn't think she could have painted anything like it.

"I take it you didn't know where Bridget and Jenny were." The painter spoke at last, frowning at Bridget. Bridget smiled back.

Samantha took a better look at him. She recognized his ginger-colored hair and mustache. This was the man the Admiral had been talking to at the circus! A closer look at his hair revealed gray streaks. He was older than she'd thought before—perhaps even as old as the Admiral—

but she felt sure this was the same man.

"Your sister has a lot of talent," the man said. "I'm glad she found me. Do the rest of you paint?" He turned kindly green eyes on Samantha.

She wanted to be angry, to scold the man the same way Nellie had scolded Bridget, but his smile was hard to resist. "Who are you?" she asked.

"Just an artist from New York City—and the world. My name is Arthur Porterfield."

Hadn't he wondered why two little girls were out here alone? "Did it occur to you, Bridget, that you and Jenny could have gotten lost?" Samantha asked.

"We weren't lost," Bridget said. "Jenny and I were right here all along. When this dries, I'm going to frame it and give it to Grandmary for her birthday."

Samantha sighed. "I'm sorry the girls were bothering you, Mr. Porterfield. But are you aware that you are on our grandmother's property?"

"The girls weren't bothering me a bit. And no one around here seems to mind my painting on their property. I'm staying at Rogers Lodge, but I ride my horse or hike all over the mountains, looking for scenes I like. Sometimes I camp overnight," Arthur Porterfield said. "I like this area so much, I'm even thinking of buying property and building a cabin as soon as the new lots go up for sale." Samantha remembered the new cabins she'd seen from the ferryboat on the way to the circus. Did Mr. Porterfield intend to build there, too?

"If you two would like to paint with Bridget and Jenny, look in my case and get some paper," the artist added as he returned to his painting.

"Thank you, but I have my own sketchbook." Samantha couldn't stay angry with Mr. Porterfield. It wasn't his fault that Bridget and Jenny had wandered off. "And we need to be heading home, or our grandmother will start worrying." Samantha turned to Jenny. "Are those Mr. Porterfield's pencils? Let's put them away now."

Reluctantly Jenny gathered up the pencils

and put them into Samantha's outstretched hand.

Samantha carried the pencils to the artist's case and opened it. It was filled with art supplies—brushes of different sizes, tubes of paint, and pads of drawing paper. But a piece of folded light brown paper caught her eye. It didn't look like drawing paper. There seemed to be printing or a diagram on it. Her mind flashed back to the scene at the circus. First the Admiral had talked to Mr. Porterfield and given him money. Then another man had given the artist a piece of light brown paper.

Curiosity overcame good manners. Samantha replaced the drawing pencils and at the same time, with her back to Arthur Porterfield, she picked up the paper, unfolded it, and stared.

It was a map of Goose Lake. Samantha was sure of it. She could even pick out the long, skinny neck of water full of dangerous rocks where her mother and father had drowned many years ago. It made sense for Mr. Porterfield to have a map, since he said that he was exploring the area looking for spots to paint. But this map was unlike any that Samantha had ever seen. Along the lake's shoreline, exactly where Piney Point was located, heavy lines of black divided the land precisely into small, tidy portions.

Tears filled Samantha's eyes. She blinked, blinked again, and brushed the tears away with the sleeve of her blouse. Had Mr. Porterfield meant that he was going to buy a piece of *Piney Point?*

7
SOMEONE IS CRYING

Quickly, Samantha refolded the map, slipped
it back into Arthur Porterfield's case, and turned
around.

"Where did you say you were building a
cabin, Mr. Porterfield?"

"Oh, that's all in the planning stage. I'd
rather not say anything until the deal goes
through. Come back tomorrow and paint with
me. I'll give you some lessons."

"Thank you. Our grandparents may have
other plans for tomorrow, though," Samantha
replied. The man seemed so nice—and yet, who
was he? Why was he painting on Grandmary's
land—and carrying that map?

Samantha bit her lip. She was sure he was
telling the truth about being an artist. His

watercolor was full of soft shades that not only captured the mountain and the meadow but made her feel the sunshine and smell the grass, the wild bluebells and the clover. But what was he doing with a map that showed Piney Point divided into little pieces?

"Good-bye, Mr. Porterfield," Samantha said. "I'll ask if we can come back and paint with you."

"Thank you for the lesson," Bridget and Jenny said together. They held their new pictures carefully by the corners to carry them safely home.

"You're welcome." Mr. Porterfield waved good-bye and turned back to his painting.

Samantha led the way down the mountain. The girls made faster progress on the return trip, but by the time they neared the lodge, the sun was sliding toward the west. Shadows had grown longer and the air cooler. The girls could see Goose Lake through the trees when Samantha signaled to stop.

"*Shhh* . . . do you hear that?" she whispered.

The girls listened hard. Nellie took Jenny's hand in hers.

THE CRY OF THE LOON

The faint sound of someone crying drifted from the woods off to the right. Samantha looked at Nellie. "Someone is in trouble. Let's go see who it is." She made her way through the trees, stepping silently on pine needles. The others followed her.

Finally she spied a figure huddled against a huge pine tree. Samantha took a step closer. It was their new maid, sobbing into her apron. "Hildy?" Samantha said softly.

Hildy looked up, her face tear-stained. "Samantha? Is that you?" She grabbed a handkerchief from her pocket, wiped her eyes, and blew her nose.

Samantha knelt down next to her. "What's wrong, Hildy? What are you doing out here alone?"

Hildy choked back a sob. "I'm so glad to see you. I think I'm lost. And—and—I started a fire at the lodge. I didn't mean to, really I didn't. It was an accident." She started crying again.

"A fire!" Samantha felt a stab of alarm. "Where? Is everyone all right?"

Hildy nodded. "Yes, yes, I think so. I was trying to do laundry. I—I've never done the wash over an open fire before. I went to hang the last load of clothes on the clothesline this afternoon, and when I turned back to the fire—oh, it was terrible. The fire under the wash pot had spread. I don't know how it happened."

Samantha was puzzled, too. During dry spells, they had to be careful that stray sparks didn't start fires on the grounds or in the woods. But there had been so much rain lately. "Did the laundry shed burn, or the guest cabins?" she asked.

"I don't know. I just don't know." Hildy shook her head and dabbed at her eyes.

"I don't smell smoke," Nellie said. "Is the fire still burning?"

"Probably not. Jack and Homer heard me screaming. They came running and started pouring buckets of water on the fire. But I was so scared, I ran—and then—then all of a sudden I wasn't sure where I was." Hildy looked down. "I didn't want to face everyone, either. I guess

I have to sooner or later, though."

Samantha's thoughts were tumbling. *Jack and Homer came running? Weren't they supposed to be off working with their father somewhere?* It seemed to Samantha that the boys must have been quite close by to have heard Hildy screaming and come running right away with buckets of water. Had they been so close by because they'd caused this "accident," too? Had they deliberately made the fire spread?

"We're not far from the lodge, Hildy. Come on, walk back with us." Samantha helped Hildy to her feet. "Let's hurry. I want to see what happened." Samantha led the way, knowing that everyone would follow her.

The area around the laundry shed was a blackened mess. The shed still stood, but the stink of scorched wood filled the air. Samantha spotted the Admiral looking around the yard with a frown on his face. Glenda was piling dirty or ruined sheets onto the floor of the laundry shed. Mr. Griffith was still pumping water, and Jack and Homer were pouring it onto the blackened grass under the clothesline and soaking the walls of the shed.

"Samantha, girls, all of you go inside," the Admiral said. "Hildy, I'll talk to you later. Right now Mrs. Hawkins needs your help." The Admiral used his *I'm-in-command* voice. Everyone jumped to follow his orders.

Mrs. Hawkins looked at the girls when they trooped through the back door. She frowned at Hildy. "Running away never solved a problem, child. Go wash your hands and face. Then come right back. I need help serving tea. Mrs. Beemis has company."

"Company? Who?" Samantha was surprised. Unexpected guests at Piney Point were rare.

"Yes, company," Mrs. Hawkins said firmly. "Now, shoo. You girls wash up quickly and join your grandmother in the dining room."

They set down their pack baskets in a corner of the kitchen and hurried to obey Mrs. Hawkins. Samantha swallowed her disappointment. She wanted to find out more about the fire, but that would have to wait.

The Cry of the Loon

As the girls approached the dining room, Samantha caught her first glimpse of the visitor. Seated at the dining table with Grandmary was a handsome man about Uncle Gard's age. He wore a green-and-black-checked flannel shirt, corduroy knickers, and hiking boots laced almost to his knees. His clothing and boots looked new. They also looked like the kind of clothes that someone from the city thought people would wear in the woods. Despite her worry about the fire, it was all Samantha could do to hide a smile.

"Prices have never been higher," the man was saying to Grandmary. "These big lodges are getting harder and harder to maintain. More and more people are selling out. That's going to cause the prices to go down, so timing is—" He stopped abruptly as the girls and Mrs. Hawkins entered the room. "Well, who have we here?" Quickly he stood up and bowed to Samantha and Nellie.

"Girls, I'd like you to meet Mr. Silas Diffenbacher," Grandmary said.

Diffenbacher… Samantha thought the name sounded familiar. Then she remembered. She'd heard it the night she eavesdropped on Grandmary and the Admiral talking about selling the lodge. This was the man who had made Grandmary an offer to buy Piney Point!

Samantha studied him as he sat down again and reached for an oatmeal cookie from the plate that Mrs. Hawkins had set on the table. Then she narrowed her eyes and looked at him more closely. For a moment, she forgot to breathe. *This* was the man she had seen talking to Arthur Porterfield at the circus, the man who had handed Mr. Porterfield a folded piece of light brown paper—surely the map she had seen in the artist's case today.

"Did you make these delicious cookies, young lady?" Mr. Diffenbacher asked Bridget.

Bridget giggled. She had crumbs all around her mouth. "No, Mrs. Hawkins made them. She's the best cook I ever knew." At a frown from Grandmary, Bridget wiped her mouth with her napkin, but her eyes were still bright.

Mr. Diffenbacher finished his cup of tea and stood up. "I have taken entirely too much of your valuable time, Mrs. Beemis. But think about what I've told you. I'll return in a week for your decision." He bowed slightly, picked up his hat, and left.

As soon as Mr. Diffenbacher had gone, Bridget and Jenny excused themselves and dashed off to the kitchen. Samantha knew the girls were eager to get their pictures and hide them until Grandmary's birthday party.

"Where does Mr. Diffenbacher live?" Nellie asked.

"I don't know, but I'm sure he's staying at one of the big hotels farther on down the lake." Grandmary smiled at both Nellie and Samantha. "Did you have fun today? Tell me everything you saw in the woods."

Nellie told Grandmary all about their day, except for the part about Bridget and Jenny running off and meeting the artist. But Samantha was silent. A lump filled her throat. She could barely keep from crying and begging her grandmother not to even *think* of selling the lodge.

"Grandmary," she finally said, "we couldn't help but hear what Mr. Diffenbacher was saying when we came in just now, about wanting to buy Piney Point and the lodge."

Grandmary sighed, and a shadow crossed her face. "I'm sorry you heard that, Samantha. I didn't want to worry you with that possibility. I don't want you to worry about it now."

"But did Mr. Diffenbacher mention what he's going to do with the property if you sell it to him?"

Grandmary was quiet for a few seconds. "If the property is his, he can do as he likes, Samantha."

Grandmary didn't say another word. Her gaze went far away, out of the dining room. Samantha wished she knew what her grandmother was thinking. But she didn't feel comfortable asking.

8
A NEAR DISASTER

Back in their room that night, Samantha and Nellie talked over the day's events. First they considered the fire. They agreed that the fire *might* have spread by itself, but they both thought it seemed awfully suspicious that—once again—Homer and Jack had been right on the scene when the latest incident happened.

Then Samantha told Nellie about the map she'd found in Mr. Porterfield's art case, and how lines on the map divided Piney Point into little pieces.

"At the circus," Samantha said, "I saw Mr. Diffenbacher give Mr. Porterfield a piece of light brown paper. And today Mr. Porterfield said that he was thinking of buying land and building a cabin around here."

"It sounds as if Mr. Diffenbacher is hoping to buy Grandmary's property so that he can divide it up and sell off the pieces," Nellie said. "And he's trying to get Mr. Porterfield to buy one of the lots."

"Grandmary doesn't seem to have made a decision about selling Piney Point yet, though," Samantha noted. "Mr. Diffenbacher said he'd be back next week for her answer."

Nellie sprawled on her bed, thinking. "Maybe," she said slowly, "we're wrong about Homer and Jack. Maybe Mr. Diffenbacher is causing the trouble so that Grandmary will want to sell Piney Point."

"But he doesn't even live here," Samantha countered. "If he's staying way off at some guest lodge or out looking for other property to buy, how could he cause trouble at Piney Point?"

Nellie blew out a frustrated breath. "I guess you're right."

"But maybe *Mr. Porterfield* could cause trouble here," Samantha said, thinking out loud. "We've seen him on the property only once, but he did say that the meadow is his favorite place to paint, and that he'd like to build a cabin around here. And he has that map."

"I still think it's more likely that Jack and Homer are causing the trouble—they can't wait to leave Piney Point, and they're always around," Nellie said. "But they *aren't* our only suspects." She got out a tablet of paper and a pencil. "Let's write down all the 'accidents' and who might have caused them."

Samantha leaned on her fist, wrinkled her brow, and started thinking. "Start your list with the boathouse, Nellie," Samantha said, counting on her fingers. "We don't know much about what happened, but Jack and Homer could have made that tree fall. They know how to use an ax and probably a saw, too."

Nellie jotted that down. "But wouldn't the Admiral have seen the ax or saw marks and realized that someone made the tree fall?" she reasoned.

"After the storm, all the men would have gone to cut up the tree. Jack and Homer could have just made sure to get there first and chop up any evidence of what they did."

Soon the girls had a list that included the tree, the dirt in the pump, the hole in the roof, the broken step, and most recently the fire. They could place Jack and Homer near each incident.

"The laundry fire was serious," Samantha said. "If it hadn't been so wet, the woods could have caught on fire, or the laundry shed, the guest cabins—even the lodge."

"That helps rule out Mr. Diffenbacher," Nellie said. "He wouldn't want the lodge to burn, because then Piney Point wouldn't be worth as much to him. Do you think Hildy might be helping Homer and Jack cause trouble? She'd like to go back to New York City, too."

"I think Hildy would have been too scared to cause the fire to spread. And she wasn't even here when the first three accidents happened." Samantha kept thinking. "Mr. Griffith was here, though. We haven't listed him," she reminded Nellie.

"But he and Glenda love living at Piney

Point. Glenda made that very clear, that they like the woods and they're glad to have a job here."

"And the Admiral says that in spite of his bad leg, Mr. Griffith is a hard worker. Jim said so, too, and Jim is a good judge of people."

Both girls were tired and out of ideas. "I know two things, Nellie," Samantha said, getting into bed. "First thing tomorrow morning, we have to keep looking for clues as to who is causing trouble. And we have to remind Grandmary how much she loves Piney Point. We have to help her decide not to sell the lodge."

At breakfast the next morning, the Admiral stretched and pushed back from the table. "Ah, nothing like a good breakfast to fuel the day. Now, you girls go get your bathing costumes on. Jim and I will get swimming lessons under way immediately."

"Swimming! Hooray!" Bridget and Jenny said together.

"I can't believe we haven't been swimming yet." Samantha jumped up. "Come on, Nellie."

In minutes, they were all headed down the path to the lake, towels in hand. Bridget and Jenny were up ahead with Jim and the Admiral, chattering with excitement. A loon called, and then another. Overhead, a woodpecker hammered, either looking for a tasty bug or just celebrating the beautiful morning.

Nellie touched Samantha's arm and pointed. Down the beach a little way, Mr. Griffith, Jack, and Homer were raking up big piles of brush. Samantha nodded and made a face. At least the boys weren't working around the boathouse.

Nellie ran to catch up with Bridget and Jenny, but Samantha hung back. She remembered other summers, when she'd spent half her time on the lake swimming, canoeing, fishing, or just lazing on the dock, wanting to spend every minute of every sunny day outside. Unlike this summer, she'd had no worries about accidents and who caused them, no concern about Grandmary selling this special place.

She caught up to the Admiral. "The boat-house looks good as new now, Admiral. Do you know why the tree fell that night? Was it windy?"

The Admiral chuckled. "If it was, I slept through it. I can sleep through most anything. Back when I was in the navy, I learned to sleep where and when I could."

Samantha had another question. "When you checked the porch steps earlier this summer, do you think you could have missed one that was weak or partly broken?"

"Well, my eyes aren't quite as good as they used to be, and it was raining for days after we got here. What are you saying, Samantha?"

"Do—do you think that someone could be *causing* all the accidents? To stir up trouble here, or to make Grandmary discouraged enough to sell Piney Point?"

The Admiral put his hand on Samantha's shoulder. "I know you're worried about your grandmother and you don't want her to sell. But the best thing you can do for her is to have fun and enjoy Piney Point as much as you always have. Leave the worrying to the grown-ups, Samantha. Now, go have fun swimming with Nellie. Jim and I will watch Bridget and Jenny."

Samantha tried to do as the Admiral suggested and stop worrying. She joined Nellie at the sandy shoreline. The water was cool, so they waded in gradually, splashing and playing, until they got used to it. "Come on, Nellie," Samantha urged, splashing water on Nellie so that she had to wade deeper to splash back.

The sun climbed higher. Nellie and Samantha swam out to a big rock and back, giving Nellie a chance to practice her swimming. Then they took a rest on the warm sand, wrapped in big soft towels.

"Let's go out in a canoe," Samantha suggested, pointing to several boats pulled up onto the shore near the boathouse. "It's easy and fun. I'll show you how to paddle." Samantha hopped to her feet and headed for the canoes.

"Jim and Mr. Griffith and I checked all the boats and canoes after the boathouse was damaged," the Admiral called as he walked toward them, leaving Jim to oversee the younger girls. "Take any of them."

"Thank you, Jim," Samantha called to Trapper Jim. He waved back.

The Admiral held the bow of their canoe steady as the two girls climbed in. "I'll sit in the back," Samantha told Nellie. "The person in the back steers. All you have to do is paddle."

"Don't go too far with Nellie just learning," the Admiral cautioned as he pushed them off.

"Yes, Admiral," Samantha said. While still in shallow water, she showed Nellie how to place her hands on the paddle. "Just dig into the water, not too deep, and pull back. Get used to paddling on either side. You're going to be good at this."

Just as Samantha had predicted, Nellie caught on quickly. "This *is* easy—and fun," she said. "Let's go faster."

Together they made the canoe zip across the sparkling water. Samantha matched her strokes to Nellie's so that they dipped and pulled at the same time.

"We're flying!" Nellie called to Samantha. The

girls paddled harder, laughing with delight. Soon, they had nearly reached the middle of the lake.

"Look behind you, Nellie," Samantha said. "You can see all of Piney Point from here." She squinted against the sun's glare. "And look, there's a big rowboat that's stopped in front of the lodge." She slowed the canoe, trying to see who might have rowed over to Piney Point. She made out a red-haired figure sitting in the boat. "Why, it's Arthur Porterfield."

The artist seemed to have a small easel propped up in the boat. He kept leaning forward to brush on paint, then leaning back again to see what he had done.

"He must be painting a picture of the lodge, Samantha. That's where he's looking as he works."

A breeze whipped over the lake, sending a tiny chill across Samantha's skin. "Didn't he say he was painting in the meadow again today? What's he doing here?" The image of the map flashed across her mind. Why was he painting their lodge?

"Let's go closer and take a look," Nellie suggested.

Samantha dipped deeper with her paddle and swung the back of the canoe around.

"Samantha," Nellie said, her voice sounding a little shaky. "Is there supposed to be water in the canoe?"

Samantha looked down. She had been resting her feet on the middle seat and hadn't noticed the film of water that now shimmered at the bottom of the canoe. "No, and it's getting deeper. Start paddling back. Fast!"

The girls tried to make the canoe skim across the lake as they had earlier, but water was coming in quickly, making the canoe heavier.

"This isn't working," Samantha said. "Quick, scoop the water out." She laid her paddle across the seats, cupped her hands, filled them with water, and flipped the water out.

She and Nellie kept scooping water as fast as they could, but Samantha realized that the water in the boat was still rising. "Help!" she called, looking back toward shore. "Help us!"

A NEAR DISASTER

Far away in the shallow water, she could see the Admiral and Trapper Jim helping Bridget and Jenny learn to swim. They didn't seem to hear Samantha and Nellie yelling.

Frantically, Samantha and Nellie scooped water, faster and faster. But the more they scooped, the more came in. The boat rode lower and lower in the water. "We're going to have to get out and tip the canoe over to keep it from sinking," Samantha said.

"I can't swim all the way back," Nellie cried. "I'm not that good a swimmer."

"Do just as I say, Nellie. Here, watch me." Samantha eased herself out of the canoe and into the lake, keeping hold of the canoe's edge. Fear filled Nellie's eyes, but she followed Samantha's example. Once in the water, she gripped the opposite edge of the canoe.

"Help!" Samantha yelled again.

To their right, they heard a voice call, "What's the matter, girls?"

9
UNEXPECTED HELP

Samantha saw Arthur Porterfield rowing his bigger boat in their direction.

He bent double and pulled toward them. "I'll swing around and get as close to you as I can," he called. "Can you grab the side of my boat and pull yourselves in? I'll try to help."

Mr. Porterfield angled his boat close to Nellie and held out a hand. Samantha saw that Nellie's face was white with fright.

"Go on, Nellie," Samantha said. "I'll help you."

Samantha took a deep breath, swam under the canoe to the other side, and boosted Nellie up and into the rowboat. Kicking to the surface, Samantha coughed and spit and regained her breath. Then she grabbed the side of Mr.

Porterfield's rowboat, pulled herself up, and tumbled into the bottom of his boat.

Just as she sank into the dry safety of the rowboat, she saw Mr. Porterfield's painting sail away. As the paper hit the lake's surface, water washed over it and the colors faded.

"Thank you for helping us," Samantha said as she settled next to Nellie, who huddled, shivering, on a long plank seat. "I'm so sorry about your painting."

The artist shook his head. "I can paint another picture. Are you girls all right? That's what's important. What happened?" He handed Nellie a jacket and gave his handkerchief to Samantha so that she could dry her face.

Samantha drew in another breath of warm, sweet air. "We—our canoe started to leak. It was filling up fast, and I couldn't get the Admiral to hear us. I'm so glad you were here."

Nellie shivered even harder, and Samantha put her arm around her, helping to keep them both warm as Mr. Porterfield rowed the heavier boat toward the Piney Point dock.

By the time they reached the dock, a whole crowd—the Admiral, Jim, Bridget, Jenny, even Jack and Homer—was waiting. Everyone but Jack and Homer looked anxious and concerned.

"I thought you girls said you knew how to paddle a canoe," Homer said, a big grin on his face.

"Maybe you need a few more lessons," Jack added. He was grinning, too.

"Why don't you two boys do something useful? Swim out and bring that canoe back," the Admiral said. He didn't seem to be in the mood for nonsense or teasing.

Samantha watched as both boys headed into the lake, swimming strongly, to retrieve the canoe.

"What happened, Samantha?" the Admiral asked. He wasn't angry, just puzzled and worried. "Are you both all right?"

"Yes, thanks to Mr. Porterfield," Samantha replied.

The Admiral reached out to shake the artist's hand. "Thank you, Arthur. I'm grateful you saw what was happening and knew that the girls needed help."

"You're entirely welcome. I'm just glad that everyone's safe." He smiled at the girls, pushed his boat back into the water, and rowed off toward the spot where he had been working.

"The canoe sprang a leak," Samantha told the Admiral when the artist had left. "Water was coming in too fast to bail it out. We had to get out before the canoe sank. We couldn't get your attention, but Mr. Porterfield saw us."

Trapper Jim frowned. "I checked the boats myself after the boathouse was damaged, and then again yesterday. There were no leaks."

"We'll take a look at the canoe when the boys get it back," the Admiral said. "Samantha, you and the girls go up to the lodge and change clothes. I know you're cold."

"I'd like to stay here," Samantha said. "I want to see what happened, too." She grabbed a big towel and wrapped herself in it, pulling it tight for warmth. She shivered and her teeth chattered, but she settled on the edge of the dock to wait.

"I'm staying with you, Samantha." Nellie wrapped up and sat on the dock. Bridget and Jenny did the same, settling on either side of her.

Soon the sun warmed them—on the outside, at least. Samantha still felt a cold lump in her stomach.

They all watched as Jack and Homer reached the canoe, then started to tow it back to shore. Bridget and Jenny, restless, left the others to play in the sand.

Keeping her voice low, Nellie said, "Remember how Jack and Homer asked us earlier if we could swim and if we knew how to canoe?"

"You don't think they made the canoe leak, do you?" Samantha whispered. She'd never imagined the boys would do something so dangerous.

As soon as Homer and Jack reached the shore, they tugged the boat out onto the sand and tipped it over so that the water could run out.

"Thank you, boys," the Admiral said. "Now, why don't you go up to your place and change into dry clothing. We'll manage from here."

Unexpected Help

Jack and Homer had no choice but to follow the Admiral's suggestion. If they were curious about the canoe, they'd have to ask their dad later what happened. *Unless they already know,* Samantha thought to herself.

Samantha and Nellie watched as Jim studied the boat and then knelt to run his hands over the sides and bottom. The Admiral crouched beside him, watching. Finally Jim said, "Look right here, Admiral. The seam opened up."

"We tested the canoe in the water yesterday, Jim." The Admiral narrowed his eyes and shook his head.

Jim nodded. "The canoe was perfect yesterday. Watertight." He stood, a grim look on his face, and turned toward the girls. "How fortunate that Mr. Porterfield was close by and heard you, Samantha."

The Admiral stood, too. "You girls have to be cold. Let's go on back to the lodge. Jim, will you see to the canoe?"

The Admiral took Bridget and Jenny's hands and started up the path, with Samantha and

Nellie right behind. "Bridget and Jenny, promise me you won't tell Grandmary about this incident," he said. He looked over his shoulder. "That goes for you too, Nellie and Samantha."

"None of us will, Admiral," Samantha said. "We don't want her worrying about us." She looked at the younger girls to make sure they understood. Bridget nodded and took off up the path. Jenny held on to the Admiral's hand.

Samantha and Nellie walked slowly, falling behind them, each lost in thought about the accident and the events of the summer. "I'm sorry, Nellie," Samantha said. "The summer isn't going at all the way I'd hoped and planned. I did so want you to love it here."

"I do love Piney Point, Samantha. I just don't like all the scary things that keep happening, but they're not your fault. And it was lucky that Mr. Porterfield was there to rescue us just now."

Samantha halted as a thought struck her. "*Was* it just a lucky coincidence, Nellie, that Arthur Porterfield was painting on the lake this morning? What is he doing painting a picture of Piney Point?" Her mind flashed back again to the map in his case. "I'll bet he's already planning where he'll build his new cabin." The thought made Samantha angry. "All the more reason for us not to tell Grandmary about the accident."

"*And* for us to figure out what's going on at Piney Point," Nellie added.

Dressed in warm, dry clothing, Samantha and Nellie hurried downstairs for lunch. To Samantha's surprise, she found she was starving. Plates stacked with sandwiches sat on the table. Another plate held fruit, and there were glasses of lemonade for everyone.

Grandmary sat at the table. Her ankle was still wrapped, but she looked more cheerful today. "The Admiral said you got too cold for the picnic I was going to send down to the lake. But otherwise, how was your morning?" Grandmary's eyes sparkled, since she was sure she knew the answer to her question.

Samantha glanced at the Admiral. "Nellie remembered how to swim in no time, Grandmary. And you should have seen her when we went out on the lake in the canoe. She caught on to paddling fast. I know we'll have a lot of fun on the lake this summer."

After lunch, Samantha announced, "We have things to do before your birthday party tomorrow, Grandmary. May we be excused?"

Grandmary's face crinkled into a smile. "I think everyone is keeping secrets. I can hardly wait to see what they are. Go on, then. The Admiral will keep me company."

Before she could decide what to do first, Samantha glanced out the window and noticed that instead of going to his cabin, Trapper Jim had started back downhill to the lake. "Nellie, I'll be up to our room in a few minutes. I want to talk to Trapper Jim."

Nellie nodded and led Bridget and Jenny upstairs.

By the time Samantha caught up to Jim, he

was squatting beside the canoe, which now sat upright on the sand. He ran his hand over the inner seams, humming as he often did while he worked and thought.

Samantha knelt beside him. "I know you thought the canoe was safe, Jim," she said.

"The canoe *was* safe." His fingers continued to explore the canoe's interior. He appeared to be checking all the seams again.

Samantha leaned closer to get a better look at the inside of the canoe. "What do you use to seal the seams?"

"Pine pitch. See?" Jim pointed to a dark brown seam that ran along each side of the bottom of the boat.

"Could the seam have come apart by itself in the water?"

"Not likely."

Samantha waited. Apparently Jim wasn't going to say what he thought happened. When she was sure that he'd finished talking about the canoe, she asked, "Jim, how would you feel if someone bought Piney Point and divided it up into pieces to sell? If more people came and built cabins here, would that mean more work for you as a guide, since those people probably wouldn't know how to hunt or fish?"

She didn't think Jim knew anything about Mr. Diffenbacher's offer or Mr. Porterfield's map. She just wanted to get his opinion.

Jim appeared to be thinking the idea over. "I might have more guide work," he said finally. "But there wouldn't be as many fish or birds. The deer would go away. There would be no more animals to hunt."

"The woods would be ruined?"

"Changed." Jim started to hum again. Samantha thought he was finished talking. But he wasn't. As she stood, he said, "Keep your eyes open, Samantha."

Samantha caught her breath. Maybe Jim had seen something he didn't want to talk about, or suspected something he couldn't prove. She waited, then finally gave up on Jim revealing anything else. "I will," she promised.

She turned to leave and then saw that Mr.

Porterfield was still out in his boat, painting.

"Jim, do you know that artist, Arthur Porterfield?"

"Sometimes I see him painting."

"Don't you think it's strange that he's painting the lodge?"

"Might be. Will you tell the Admiral I'd like to talk to him?" Jim got up and headed for the storage shed on the dock.

If Jim knew more than he was saying, he wasn't going to share it with Samantha, but surely he was going to tell the Admiral. Maybe then the Admiral wouldn't think Samantha's imagination was running away with her. Maybe he'd take a second look at *all* the accidents that had happened this summer around the lodge.

10
THE LEAN-TO CAMP

By the time Samantha had walked back to the lodge, she'd come up with an idea. She hurried upstairs and found Nellie playing with Bridget and Jenny and their dollhouse.

"Nellie, I need you to help me with some work," Samantha said.

At the mention of work, Bridget and Jenny were happy to play alone for a little while.

"What work?" Nellie asked once they'd stepped outside the back door.

Samantha started across the backyard as she explained. "I got to thinking about how Mr. Porterfield said he sometimes camps near the place where he's painting. We saw him around Piney Point late yesterday afternoon and then again this morning. There's a camp on the edge of Grandmary's property. I want to go see it, to see if Mr. Porterfield has been staying there."

"Should we tell someone where we're going?" Nellie asked as Samantha set off along a forest path, leaving the stink of the recent fire behind them. "It looks as if it's going to storm."

"We won't be gone long. No one will miss us."

Despite dark clouds gathering, birds sang high overhead. Pine trees grew close along the path, forming a thick canopy overhead so that very little light reached the ground. A raven croaked with its raspy voice. The sound sent a shiver through Samantha. Neither she nor Nellie liked ravens. Nellie said they were bad luck.

As they neared the camp at the edge of Grandmary's property, all sound seemed to stop. Nerves tingling, Samantha listened harder, but she heard nothing—not even the sound of their own cautious footsteps, silenced by the carpet of pine needles.

On tiptoe, the girls circled around a thicket of scrub oak and cedar trees. Through the trees, they could see the camp—a lean-to shelter set in a clearing—and farther beyond through the trees, the flat gray sheen of the lake. Samantha put out her hand, and both girls stood quietly for a short time. Still hearing nothing, they stepped into the clearing and approached the lean-to. It was made of small spruce logs that sloped up to an overhanging roof.

Just outside the crude shelter, a circle of large blackened rocks held the remains of a fire. An iron pot hung over the fireplace. Nellie stepped closer.

"Someone has been camping here, Samantha. This pot still has food in it."

"But is it Mr. Porterfield who's staying here? Let's look around." Peering into the lean-to, Samantha saw fishing and hunting gear hanging on the walls. The plank floor was bare except for a pile of fragrant balsam branches piled in one corner. They were covered with blankets to make a rough bed.

"I don't see any painting supplies," Samantha whispered. "But maybe Mr. Porterfield would have taken them with him on the lake."

Nellie leaned in next to Samantha and studied the interior of the shelter. "Do you think Jack and Homer might be camping out here sometimes?" she suggested.

"I don't think so, Nellie. Look over there." Samantha pointed to a new-looking leather jacket hanging on a peg in one corner. "That seems too expensive for the boys to own."

Thunder rumbled, and Samantha saw that thick clouds were building up over the lake. Even though it was early afternoon, the woods were getting dark.

"We'd better go back, or we'll get soaked for the second time today," Samantha said. "Besides, someone has been here recently, and he may be coming back ahead of the storm."

They slipped into the woods and didn't speak again until they were well away from the camp.

Finally, Samantha broke the silence. "Even though I didn't see any art supplies in the lean-to, I think it must be Mr. Porterfield who's camping there. We've seen a lot of him lately.

I wonder, Nellie—if he *is* staying at the camp, it wouldn't be hard for him to slip over to the lodge and cause mischief, hoping to push Grandmary to sell. Maybe we've been too quick to judge Jack and Homer."

Nellie considered that. "I don't know. It's possible, but Mr. Porterfield seems so nice. He was so kind to Bridget and Jenny yesterday, and to us, too. And he did say that he camps near his favorite places so that he can paint them. Maybe that's the truth."

In the distance, Samantha heard another rumble of thunder. She quickened her pace. "Yes, but Nellie, think of this. We know, or at least we're pretty sure, it was no accident that our canoe swamped. And afterward, Jim told me to keep my eyes open. That tells me he is suspicious of someone. Maybe Mr. Porterfield sneaked over last night and did something to the canoe, but he didn't really want anyone to get hurt—he only meant to frighten us, or to frighten Grandmary. So this morning, he made sure he was close enough to rescue us."

Nellie looked doubtfully at Samantha. "It's possible, Samantha, but I just don't want to think it of him. Besides, how could he know that we'd take the canoe out this morning? And it still seems as if Homer and Jack are the ones who are always around when things go wrong."

Samantha had to admit that Nellie made a good argument against Mr. Porterfield being the troublemaker. Samantha wasn't sure what to think.

"I guess we just have to keep looking and listening for anything suspicious and adding to our list. Come on." Samantha grabbed Nellie's hand as another peal of thunder cracked. "We'd better run."

Sprinkles of rain had started to fall by the time the girls got back to the lodge. Bridget and Jenny came running to greet them. "Where were you?" asked Bridget. "We got tired of playing by ourselves."

Samantha and Nellie looked at each other. "We went for a walk," Nellie said. "But now let's get ready for Grandmary's birthday party tomorrow evening."

"I have a wonderful idea for a centerpiece to put on the dining table," Samantha said. "Let's work on it in the attic. Grandmary told me a long time ago that the attic could be my special place at Piney Point. But first, girls, remember all those pinecones you put in the pack baskets when we had our picnic? Do you know where they are?"

"They're still in the baskets," Bridget said. "Mrs. Hawkins asked us to move the baskets from the kitchen to our room. So we did."

In no time, they had carried the baskets up the steep flight of stairs that led to the attic. As they entered the long, narrow room with its dim light and dusty corners, rain rattled on the roof and slid down the windows.

Bridget's eyes got big. "Look at all the boxes to explore. Is it all right, Samantha?"

"Yes, there are boxes of old clothing and hats. You can play dress-up. And there's a box of games, too. But first, let's make the centerpiece for Grandmary. She loves loons, so I thought we could make loons for her out of pinecones."

"How do you make a loon out of a pinecone, Samantha?" Jenny asked.

"I'll show you my idea. Help me put the pinecones on the table and pick out the biggest ones." Samantha got out paper, scissors, glue, paints, and crayons. She spread them out on a table she often used for projects. From a sheet of stiff black paper, she cut out the profile of a loon's head with its long, daggerlike bill.

"Loons are mostly black, but the neck has a white band and the back is spotted with white. We can paint the pinecones and then glue on the neck and head. At the very last, we'll use dabs of red paint for the loons' eyes." Quickly Samantha drew a picture of a loon on a separate piece of paper so that they'd have a pattern.

"You must have looked at loons for a long time to see all that detail," said Nellie as she studied the picture.

"Last summer I was alone a lot, so I did

watch them. I kept getting closer and closer, as close as they'd allow." Samantha picked up a pinecone. "And sometimes Grandmary and I watched together."

"How about feet?" Bridget asked.

"Our loons will be swimming," Samantha said. "I don't think I've ever seen a loon's feet." She smiled at Bridget.

"Should we make a nest?" Jenny asked.

"Grandmary would probably rather not have a pile of grass on the table." Samantha laughed at the idea. "And we have to leave room for presents."

When all four girls had made a loon, they set them in the middle of the work table. "See how wonderful they look?" Samantha was pleased that her idea had turned out so well.

"Now, Bridget, you and Jenny can explore the attic. I want to show Nellie my mother's sketch-book." Samantha loved the pictures her mother had drawn during her own summers at Piney Point. Together, Samantha and Nellie knelt by a dusty box in the corner. Samantha gently lifted out the familiar maroon sketchbook.

"Your mother was a real artist," Nellie said, turning pages in the book. "Look, this is you when you were little."

Samantha nodded, wishing that she could remember being here with her mother and father.

Before Samantha could get too sad about the past, Jenny held out her hand. "Look what I found, Samantha. Isn't it pretty?"

Samantha took the heart-shaped gold locket that Jenny held out. It was lovely and reminded Samantha of her own locket, which held a picture of her parents.

"Open it," Jenny urged. "Look inside."

Samantha snapped the locket open and caught her breath. Staring back at her was a tiny but exquisitely detailed painting of a beautiful young woman.

"Who is it?" Bridget asked.

"It's not my mother." Samantha studied the portrait of the gray-eyed beauty. "I—I think it might be Grandmary."

Nellie held the locket and looked closer. "I think you're right."

"Where did you find it?" Samantha asked Jenny.

Jenny pointed to the open box. "In there."

Samantha knelt by the box again. "These are my mother's things. This is where I first found the sketchbook we were looking at, Nellie. I'll bet Grandmary has forgotten all about this locket. We'll give it to her on her birthday."

Nellie looked at the painting in the locket again. "She was beautiful."

"She still is." Samantha stood next to Nellie and studied the portrait. "Grandmary and her family have been coming to Piney Point every summer since my mother and Uncle Gard were little. What a shame it would be to never come here again."

Nellie squeezed Samantha's hand. "We'll work together, Samantha. We'll keep trying to discover who is causing all the trouble at Piney Point."

11
SPECIAL TIME
WITH GRANDMARY

Samantha put the locket into her pocket and left the pinecone loons to bring down tomorrow for Grandmary's birthday party.

"I'm going to read to Bridget and Jenny before dinner," Nellie said. "Are you coming, Samantha?"

"Go ahead. I have so much on my mind, I don't think I can be still, even with one of your good stories." Samantha smiled. Nellie was so good at taking care of her little sisters. Samantha hoped she could be as good at helping with her new cousin, William Samuel. He was going to be like her little brother.

As her sisters settled into Bridget and Jenny's room to read, Samantha went downstairs. The house seemed deserted. She looked into the kitchen. Good smells suggested that dinner was in the oven. Mrs. Hawkins must have been taking a rare few minutes off, maybe taking a nap herself. Samantha didn't see Hildy anywhere, or the Admiral and Jim.

She stepped outside and looked around at the backyard. The rain had ended, leaving behind a misty fog, which brought out the smell of burnt grass. She walked out into the yard and past the icehouse, but she saw only Jack and Homer near the Griffiths' cottage, visiting with Hildy as they hoed weeds in their mother's garden. Samantha turned back to the lodge in time to see Mr. Griffith limping along, carrying a ladder. He leaned it on the wall of the storage shed. He must have been concentrating on the work he had to do, Samantha thought, since he didn't even notice her slip past him.

There was still no one in the kitchen, but she had been gone only a few minutes. Wandering into the living room, she looked out the front windows. She spotted Grandmary, alone on the front porch. Did she want to be alone?

Samantha stepped outside. "Do you mind having company, Grandmary?" she asked. The air felt chilly, and Samantha rubbed her arms.

"Not at all, dear." Grandmary smiled and gestured at a tea tray on a wicker side table. "Come and pour yourself a cup of cocoa. Mrs. Hawkins made a pot in case you girls happened along."

As Samantha filled a cup and settled into a chair next to Grandmary, a loon's call floated up from the lake: *Ooo–oooo, ooo–oooo, ooo–oooo.* The loons seemed to talk more when the weather was foggy. Another loon from farther away answered the first loon with a yodeling cry. Samantha sat quietly, listening. The quiet time reminded her of other, more peaceful summers.

Ooo–oooo, ooo–oooo, ooo–oooo.

"They have four different calls," Grandmary said, setting her teacup down with a clink on the saucer. "Jim taught me to hear all four last summer."

"Is that the mother and the father talking?" Samantha asked.

"The female stays quiet while she's on the nest," Grandmary said. "If the male goes to get food for her, they stay in touch with little hoots like an owl's. That trembling, laughterlike call is probably one male talking to another. He's saying, 'This nesting spot is taken. This female is taken. Go find your own.'"

Samantha smiled, surprised that Grandmary, who was usually so proper, would talk about two male loons quarreling over one female. But what she said made Samantha remember the locket and how beautiful Grandmary's portrait was. She felt brave enough to ask a question about when Grandmary was young.

"Did two young men ever compete over you, Grandmary?"

"Oh, dear," Grandmary said. "I opened the door to that question, didn't I?" She poured a second cup of tea, lifted it halfway to her lips, and paused for the longest time.

Samantha kept quiet, waiting. She sipped her hot chocolate, enjoying its warmth and bittersweet taste. She took a deep breath of the misty, pine-scented air, closed her eyes, and tried not to think about anything except this quiet time with Grandmary.

When Grandmary continued, there was a smile in her voice. "I had many gentlemen callers when I was young. The custom was to have big parties so that young ladies could meet young men. It didn't take long for me to know that two young men were special. And both made it clear they liked me."

"Were they both tall and handsome?" Samantha couldn't resist asking.

"Yes. They were very different, but both were handsome and charming, and made me laugh. It's important that a young man can make you laugh, Samantha."

A couple of years ago, Samantha couldn't have imagined having such a conversation with Grandmary. Samantha had been almost afraid of her grandmother then, because she was so quiet and stern and because she hardly ever smiled. Perhaps, Samantha realized now, Grandmary had been sad all that time. Sad to have lost her daughter and then Grandfather. Now the Admiral was making her happy again.

"So how did you choose between the two suitors?" Samantha asked.

"One was charming and always having fun, but I realized he was rather irresponsible. He wasn't sure what he was going to do with his life. He had no plan for his future, our future."

"And the other? Was that Grandfather?" Samantha guessed.

"Yes. Maybe he didn't laugh as much, but he talked to me. All the time. He told me his plans for going to college, then plans for his career. And he'd ask what I thought. He welcomed my ideas. Most women expected only to get married and have a family, but he wanted to know what kind of plans I had.

"After we were married, we'd talk every night after dinner. He'd ask my opinion about a business deal. I'd help him think it over. He usually followed my advice or made me see why his idea was better. We made a good team. Soon William's business made enough money that we could buy Piney Point."

"That was a long time ago, wasn't it? When my mother and Uncle Gard were children."

Grandmary nodded. "We bought the land, and I drew up plans for the main lodge as we talked over everything we wanted. The other buildings sprouted up like weeds, or hickory saplings."

"Did you ever see the other young man again?"

"No, I didn't. I've often wondered what he went on to do or be—if he had a successful career and a family."

They sat in silence for a few minutes. The loon called out again. "I'm glad you and Grandfather bought Piney Point. I can't imagine our family without it," Samantha dared to say.

Grandmary looked thoughtfully at Samantha. "I'd always planned to leave Piney Point to your mother and Gard, now to Gard and Cornelia, of course. And I imagined that someday, Samantha, Piney Point would belong to you, Nellie and the girls, and little William."

They sat thinking again, enjoying the quiet

and each other's company. Samantha realized that for the first time, Grandmary had talked to her as she would talk to an adult.

She didn't want to ask any more questions. She didn't want to ask Grandmary if she'd made a decision about selling. She wanted this moment to last forever.

The silence didn't last, of course. Nellie, Bridget, and Jenny stepped out the front door. "There you are, Samantha," Bridget said. "Mrs. Hawkins told us to find you. Dinner is ready. Aren't you starved? Can we have chocolate pudding first, Grandmary? May we?"

Grandmary smiled. "Of course not, dear. You have to eat all your dinner—vegetables too. Eating dessert first would never be proper."

The proper Grandmary was back, but her voice held a teasing note that Samantha was glad to hear. Maybe she'd helped put it there. Maybe she'd helped Grandmary think about some plans for the future.

12
GRANDMARY'S BIRTHDAY PARTY

The next day dawned with no rain, but the air remained damp and cool. Samantha felt that not even a little rain could spoil Grandmary's birthday party. This was such a special day!

As soon as breakfast was finished, all the girls got busy making blue and white paper chains to hang in the dining and living rooms. The Admiral and Jim brought in big bouquets of wildflowers, which Hildy helped to arrange in two vases.

"Good job, girls," the Admiral said. "The day is sailing ahead splendidly, and to top it off, we have a surprise visitor coming."

"Who, Admiral?" Samantha asked. She couldn't imagine who the visitor could be. It couldn't be any of Grandmary's friends from

Mount Bedford, because none of the guest cabins had been aired out. "Surely not Uncle Gard and—"

"No, unfortunately, they still aren't able to travel. Just wait and see." The Admiral smiled and hurried away.

As Samantha and Nellie hung decorations, they made silly guesses about who might visit. Then Nellie paused as she draped a paper chain over a windowsill. "Samantha," she whispered, "come here. Isn't that Mr. Porterfield heading down to the lake?"

Samantha joined Nellie at the window. "It's Mr. Porterfield, but I don't see his boat at the dock, and surely he wouldn't be going out on the lake to paint with rain threatening. Let's go see what he's doing."

Samantha and Nellie slipped out the front door and down the porch steps. They stayed among the trees instead of using the path and got to the lake just in time to see Arthur Porterfield glance around as if to check that no one was watching. Then he walked across the dock to the boathouse. With another furtive glance around, the artist slipped inside.

Staying hidden in the woods, the girls waited to see what would happen next. A fine mist began to fall, and Samantha wished that she had a jacket. She and Nellie huddled down behind a massive pine tree, making themselves as small as possible.

"It's strange that he would be in the boathouse at all," Samantha murmured. "What could he be doing? I wish we could sneak up and peek in the window." Samantha found it hard to be still and wait, but she felt that they must.

Finally the boathouse door opened and the artist reappeared. "Look," Nellie said. "Now he's carrying a package."

They watched as Mr. Porterfield headed up the path and around to the back of the lodge. "Let's go see if we can tell what he was doing," Samantha said. The girls hurried to the boathouse, but when they reached it, they found a padlock on the door. The boathouse was locked up tight. Samantha shot a worried look at Nellie.

"He must have a key to our boathouse. How on earth could Mr. Porterfield have gotten a key?"

"I hate to think he stole it," Nellie said. "What's in the boathouse?"

"It's where the Admiral and Jim store boats, canoes, extra paddles, and tools." Samantha swallowed hard, wondering if he had slipped into the boathouse just this way to tamper with the canoe. Was another "accident" pending now? Samantha saw that Nellie's eyes were filled with worry, too.

"Well, we can't get inside the boathouse," Samantha said. "We'd better get back to the lodge before someone misses us."

They hurried back to the lodge, still puzzling over the artist's actions.

After a light lunch of sandwiches and cocoa, Mrs. Hawkins said the four girls could set the dining table for the party while Grandmary was resting. "Choose a pretty tablecloth, girls, and set the table for eight. Use Grandmary's best dishes, but handle them carefully."

"We will. And we need our centerpiece," Samantha said. "Bridget and Jenny, you go get the loons."

"All right." Jenny tried to keep up with Bridget as they both ran up the stairs.

In the sideboard, Samantha sorted through tablecloths. "Oh, look at this one, Nellie. It's the same color as the scarf I bought in the village for Grandmary." She pulled out the light blue cloth.

She and Nellie spread the cloth on the table. Samantha knew that one set of Grandmary's dishes was white with a blue rim, the sky blue color that was Grandmary's favorite.

After the dishes and silverware were in place, the girls arranged the pinecone loons in the center of the table. "I wish we'd made a baby loon," Bridget said. "Why didn't we think of that? I saw a lot of small pinecones."

"The centerpiece is beautiful," Nellie assured her. "And there has to be room for presents and birthday cake. Now, we'd better go get changed into our prettiest dresses." Nellie led the way upstairs.

By the time the girls got back to the dining room, their hands full of presents, Trapper Jim was bringing in an armload of wood. He stirred the fire to a lively crackle. "Very pretty decorations for the house and the table, girls," Jim said. "Good job."

"Thank you, Jim," Samantha said as she, Nellie, and the girls placed their colorful packages on the dining table.

"What a grand-looking table!" the Admiral boomed from the hallway. Samantha turned to greet him, then blinked twice to be sure her eyes weren't deceiving her. With the Admiral, acting as if they were old friends, was Mr. Porterfield. He had changed from his old painting clothes into a handsome suit. His hair and mustache were perfectly groomed, and his green eyes twinkled.

This was the surprise guest? Samantha and Nellie looked at each other, astonished.

Quickly, Samantha remembered her manners. "Hello, Mr. Porterfield. Did you paint another picture of the lodge after we ruined your first one?"

"I did indeed, thank you. I'm glad to see you girls looking none the worse for—"

"*Shhh*," Samantha warned. Grandmary had just come downstairs, and Samantha didn't want her to hear about the boating disaster. A quick glance at Grandmary's smiling face as she entered the room told Samantha that she hadn't heard a thing. But when Samantha looked back at Arthur Porterfield, she saw that his face had turned pale.

"My dear," the Admiral said to Grandmary, "I don't think you've met our resident artist. This is Arthur Porterfield. Mr. Porterfield, my wife, Mary Beemis."

"How do you do, Mr. Porterfield? I believe I did see you painting on the lake. I hope I'll have the opportunity to see the results someday."

"I'm sure you will," Mr. Porterfield said. He bowed to Grandmary and kissed her hand as if she were the Queen of Piney Point. Grandmary gave a delighted little laugh.

Samantha couldn't help but giggle. She

turned to Nellie, whose eyes were wide with surprise, too. They grinned at each other and shrugged. They would make the artist welcome, at least for today. But they would watch him carefully.

Grandmary played the piano for a little while. Nellie entertained the girls by teaching them to play cat's cradle. But Samantha found herself paying close attention to Mr. Porterfield. He chatted with the Admiral and Jim, but his eyes were more often on Grandmary, and he seemed uncomfortable.

When it was finally time for dinner and everyone was seated at the big dining table, Samantha noticed that Mr. Porterfield, seated beside Jim, leaned back, as if he was shy and hoped he wouldn't have to talk. *How odd*, Samantha thought. *He never seemed shy or quiet before.* The table fell silent for a few minutes as Mrs. Hawkins, Glenda, and Hildy served broth, then gathered the soup bowls and served a delicious roast of venison with browned potatoes and carrots.

GRANDMARY'S BIRTHDAY PARTY

Samantha noticed that Grandmary didn't eat a great deal, as if she was saving room for dessert. Her eyes smiled at Samantha when Grandmary caught her watching. "The centerpiece is lovely, girls," Grandmary said. "What a creative idea, and you know I love the loons."

"That was Samantha's idea," Nellie said.

"But we all helped." Bridget beamed at Samantha, making her glad again that the three girls were a part of her family. "I wish we had thought to make a baby loon, though."

"Speaking of babies, I wonder how little William is faring. I know that Gard and Cornelia made the right decision not to come this summer, but I'm missing them all the same." Grandmary glanced at the Admiral. "Not that I don't have wonderful company here, but William will have grown so much by the time we see him again."

When dinner was finished and the table cleared, Hildy entered, carrying a cake alight with candles.

"There's the cake!" Jenny clapped her hands. "Look how many candles Grandmary has."

"Oh, you shouldn't have, Mrs. Hawkins," Grandmary said. "We're going to start a fire." Quickly Grandmary motioned to Bridget and Jenny to join her, and the three blew out all the candles at once.

"Are you only sixteen?" Bridget finished counting the candles and grinned.

"Maybe each candle counts for two," Jenny said, looking as if she was trying to figure out how many years that would be.

The Admiral let out a booming laugh. "I think you need to give Jenny a slice of cake, Mrs. Hawkins, before she gets into trouble," he said, winking at Grandmary.

Everyone lingered over coffee and cocoa, reluctant to end the lovely dinner. Samantha looked around the table, grateful that Nellie, Bridget, and Jenny could be here for a summer. If this was their last party at Piney Point, at least they'd have good memories. Then, finally, she couldn't stand the suspense any more. "Isn't it time for your presents, Grandmary?"

"Presents? All this lovely dinner, cake, and

presents, too? My, my, I am going to get spoiled."

Samantha handed a colorful package to Grandmary. "This one is from Uncle Gard and Aunt Cornelia," she said. "Open it first."

Grandmary tore off the paper carefully, then caught her breath as she gazed at the framed picture inside. "Oh, look at this." She turned the frame around and showed them a photograph of the happy new family. Snuggled between mother and father was the smiling baby, William. Grandmary passed the photograph around the table so that everyone could have a closer look. "I'm so pleased. They're here in spirit."

No one could top that present, but Bridget tried. "Open mine next, Grandmary." She pointed hers out.

Grandmary unfolded what looked suspiciously like one of Mrs. Hawkins's dish towels, revealing Bridget's painting. "Oh, this is lovely, Bridget. Did you paint this yourself?"

"Yes." Bridget glanced in Arthur Porterfield's direction. "But Mr. Porterfield helped me. I hope you like it."

"I recognize my favorite meadow at Piney Point. I remember hiking there when I was young. I like the painting very much, Bridget. Thank you. I'm proud of you."

Jenny held her picture out to Grandmary. "My picture isn't as good, but I was in the meadow, too."

"Look at the wildflowers. Both of your pictures are lovely. I'll hang them where I can see them every day."

While Grandmary was looking at the girls' pictures, Samantha had seen the Admiral slip out of the room. When he returned, he had his hands behind his back. "And these are for the living room." He placed three framed paintings on the cleared table in front of Grandmary. "Mind you, I didn't paint these. I asked Mr. Porterfield to paint three pictures for you, Mary."

"Oh, my," Grandmary whispered. "They're perfect." She bent close to study the paintings and then held each one up in turn so that everyone could see them. Each of the three watercolors was framed with weathered wood.

The first one was a scene in the meadow, the second showed the pine-clad Goose Lake shoreline, complete with loons, and the third was of Piney Point lodge, viewed from the lake. Samantha realized that *that* was the scene Mr. Porterfield had painted from his rowboat.

All three paintings were so lovely, they took Samantha's breath away. She felt foolish to have been so suspicious of Mr. Porterfield. She and Nellie exchanged embarrassed glances. The Admiral must have told Mr. Porterfield he could hide the pictures in the boathouse until the party. That was why he was there earlier, with a key—to get the paintings and bring them to the lodge.

"Mr. Porterfield is a well-known artist," the Admiral told Grandmary, "but I hadn't met him until we went to the village for the circus. He had a painting displayed for sale and a portfolio of other work he had done. What a lucky day that was, since I didn't know what to get for your birthday this year, Mary."

"Why didn't you tell us, Admiral, about the

paintings?" The question slipped out before Samantha could stop herself.

The Admiral laughed. "My apologies, Samantha, but I wasn't sure you and the girls could keep this secret."

Grandmary glanced at Arthur Porterfield and then looked at his paintings again. "These are very special, Archie, Mr. Porterfield. I can't thank you enough."

Samantha wished she had given her presents to Grandmary sooner. *A handkerchief and a scarf aren't nearly as exciting as the paintings,* she thought as she handed her first package to her grandmother.

Grandmary opened it and fingered the embroidery on the handkerchief. "This is lovely work, Samantha. You've become much better at sewing. Remember your first try at embroidery?" Grandmary smiled at Samantha, making her present as special as any other she had received.

"Nellie and I picked out this one together," Samantha said as she handed the other package to Grandmary. "I think it's your favorite color."

Grandmary pulled the scarf from the wrapping paper. "It is indeed. This shade of blue reminds me of the skies at Piney Point, but also of the bluebells in the meadow, and someone's eyes." She looked at the Admiral and smiled. The Admiral smiled back.

Nellie set her gift on the table next. "I got these for you at the circus," she explained after Grandmary had unwrapped the box of maple-sugar candies. "Samantha thought you'd enjoy them."

"Thank you, Nellie. I am partial to maple sugar. I wish we had our own maple trees. These look delicious."

Grandmary leaned back and glanced around the table. "Thank you all for a lovely birthday party, and these very special gifts. I am almost speechless."

The Admiral laughed at that. He and Grandmary spent many hours talking together. Samantha had often wondered how they found so much to talk about.

"There's just one more thing, Grandmary,"

Samantha said, taking the locket out of her pocket and moving beside her grandmother. "I think this is yours, but I wonder if you've forgotten all about it. We found it in the attic."

Grandmary took the necklace, hesitated, then snapped the locket open. She looked at it for a long moment, and then tears filled her eyes. "I thought I had lost this," she murmured.

"That's you, isn't it, Grandmary?" Samantha asked. "I know it is. You were beautiful. You're still beautiful, of course, but..."

"But I am just a little older than when this was painted." Grandmary smiled.

"Who painted the portrait, Grandmary?" Nellie asked.

Arthur Porterfield cleared his throat, pushed back his chair, and stood up. "I believe I did. Hello again, Mary."

"Altus?" Grandmary looked at Arthur Porterfield. "Altus Potter? Is that you? After all these years? And you've changed your name?"

"I chose a name I thought was more suited to a painter. I recognized you immediately, but I knew you didn't remember me. What a pleasure to find you again." Mr. Porterfield walked around the table. Grandmary stood up, and the portrait artist from so long ago took both her hands in his.

Samantha looked at Nellie. Smiles spread across their faces.

"You *know* Mr. Porterfield?" the Admiral asked, his blue eyes wide.

"We were—we were good friends once." Grandmary's cheeks were pink, and she looked like the shy young woman that she had been long ago.

The other man, Samantha thought. *This must be the other man who had courted Grandmary.* She could hardly wait to tell Nellie the rest of the story.

Before anyone could say more, a loud roar filled the room. Flames burst from the fireplace and raced across the floor.

13
A LIGHT IN THE WOODS

Hildy, who was serving, screamed. Trapper Jim grabbed the pitcher of water that sat on the table and poured it on the flames, but they flashed higher. Mrs. Hawkins and Glenda ran to the kitchen and returned with buckets of water. The Admiral and Mr. Porterfield grabbed the buckets and tossed water on the fire.

Grandmary turned to Samantha and Nellie. "Run!" she ordered. "Get Bridget and Jenny outside."

Samantha grabbed Jenny's hand, and Nellie took hold of Bridget's. They pushed around the table and into the kitchen, then dashed into the yard, with Grandmary following. Once outside, Samantha started to shake. Was the lodge going to burn to the ground?

Grandmary gathered all the girls around her, not speaking but hugging them close.

Once Samantha calmed down a little, she saw Burl Griffith in the twilight, already pumping water at the pump house. Jack and Homer passed sloshing buckets to the line that Mrs. Hawkins, Hildy, Jim, and Mr. Porterfield had formed to get water into the dining room and onto the fire.

"Quick," the Admiral yelled, taking charge. He pointed to a tall ladder leaning against the house. "Homer and Jack, you boys are agile. Climb that ladder and take water to the roof. Soak the shingles around the chimney to make sure the roof doesn't catch fire."

Finally, Trapper Jim and Mr. Porterfield came outside to report that the fire was out. Samantha glanced at her sisters and then looked at Grandmary, who stood with her hands on her hips, frowning. Samantha thought each of them was all right—scared or angry, perhaps, but all right. So without calling attention to herself, she slipped back inside the lodge.

A sharp acrid smell filled the dining room. The braided rug that lay in front of the fireplace was a soggy, blackened mess. Water had soaked the wooden floor, but Mrs. Hawkins and Hildy were already mopping.

"What a mess," Mrs. Hawkins muttered under her breath, but loudly enough that Samantha could hear. "Not a lot of damage, but what a mess."

"Mrs. Hawkins," Samantha said. Mrs. Hawkins swung around. She looked surprised to find Samantha inside. "Can you tell what made the fireplace blow up like that?" Samantha asked.

"That's nothing for you to worry about, Samantha," Mrs. Hawkins said, a grim look on her face. "You'd best go back outside and stay with your grandmother."

"She's all right. What would you guess caused the fire?" Samantha persisted.

Mrs. Hawkins sighed. "Don't you smell the kerosene?" She pointed to a charred pine knot that had rolled into the room and been wet down before the fire could burn it completely. A few shreds of blackened cloth clung to it. "It looks to me as if that pine knot was wrapped in rags and soaked with kerosene, and then someone threw it down the chimney. The kerosene hitting the flames is what caused the explosion. We're lucky to have gotten the fire put out so quickly. Someone didn't expect that."

"So the fire was no accident," Samantha said. She wasn't at all surprised.

"That's for certain," Mrs. Hawkins agreed. She attacked the wet floor with her mop, twisting water from the strings into a bucket.

"Does the Admiral know? Will you tell him what you told me?"

"I'll stay right here until you send him in," Mrs. Hawkins said.

Samantha ran back outside. "Admiral, Mrs. Hawkins needs to talk to you. She's in the dining room." The Admiral hurried into the lodge.

It seemed as if no one knew what to do now that the emergency was over. Samantha joined Nellie, who hugged Bridget and Jenny close together in front of her. Jim and Mr. Porterfield stood on either side of Grandmary. Mr. Griffith, his arm around Glenda, stood near the pump house, while Homer, Jack, and Hildy leaned against the laundry shed. No one spoke. They waited for the Admiral or Grandmary to tell them what to do.

The Admiral reappeared in minutes. "I think it's safe for all of you to come inside. We have to decide what to do. Burl, will you and the boys check to make sure that no one is on the grounds? Glenda, I think Mrs. Hawkins would appreciate your help in the kitchen. We could all use a strong cup of tea."

Inside, the Admiral continued to take charge, first showing Grandmary, Jim, and Mr. Porterfield the pine knot and explaining how the fire had been started.

"Don't you think we should send someone into the village to get the sheriff, Archie?" Grandmary asked.

"I'll send Mr. Griffith first thing in the morning. But tonight, I think it's safest for all of us to stay together in the lodge. Jim and Arthur will stay here, too."

"Is it safe for the girls to sleep upstairs?" Grandmary asked.

"I've checked over the entire lodge. Thanks to everyone's fast work, the fire damaged only the dining-room floor. The girls' bedrooms are fine."

Grandmary turned to Samantha, Nellie, and the younger girls. "I know all of you were frightened, but if the Admiral says we're safe here, then we are." Grandmary looked around. "Hildy, will you ask Mrs. Hawkins to make a pot of cocoa and bring it upstairs to the girls' rooms? Samantha and Nellie, I'd like you stay with Bridget and Jenny until they're asleep."

"Yes, Grandmary, we can do that," Samantha said. She took Jenny's hand, while Nellie put her arm around Bridget. The foursome made their way upstairs slowly and did as Grandmary asked.

Soon Nellie fell asleep, but Samantha lay in her bed, listening to the soft murmurs of conversation downstairs. She tried to make some sense of what had happened, but her mind tumbled with confusion, worry, and exhaustion. Finally she drifted into a dreamless sleep.

The sky was still dark when Nellie shook her awake. "Hurry, Samantha, wake up. I had a bad dream and couldn't go back to sleep, so I was looking out the window. There's somebody sneaking around outside." Samantha sat up and rubbed her eyes.

"Come look," Nellie whispered urgently.

Shoulder to shoulder, the girls peered out the window. A shadowy figure was moving stealthily across the backyard. As it neared the woods, the figure straightened, switched on a pocket torch, and began to move faster. Now Samantha could tell that it was a man—a man who walked with an odd, choppy gait. "It's Mr. Griffith, Nellie," she said. "See how he's limping?"

When Mr. Griffith had nearly reached a path that led off into the woods, he stopped, glanced all around, and then took off into the trees, almost running.

Samantha's heart pounded. "He's up to something. We need to follow him. Should we wake the Admiral or Jim?"

Nellie bit her lip. "We're supposed to stay up here. And I suppose it's possible that Mr. Griffith is just checking the grounds. Let's see what's going on first. If we see anything wrong, we'll come back and get help."

Quickly, both girls dressed and grabbed pocket torches from their dresser, hoping that Mr. Griffith didn't have too much of a head start.

Ooo–oooo, ooo–oooo, ooo–oooo, a loon called as they opened the back door quietly and slipped outside. Samantha shivered and hoped the call wasn't an omen of danger. But she was suddenly so sure that Burl Griffith was up to no good, she felt they had to follow him.

A full moon, sliding toward the west, played hide-and-seek with clouds and trees. The girls didn't see anyone outside, but they stayed in the shadow of the laundry shed and the icehouse just in case. Then Nellie pointed out the path Mr. Griffith had taken.

"It's the path that leads to the lean-to camp," Samantha whispered.

Samantha set out down the path. As her eyes adjusted to the deeper darkness of the woods, she moved silently through the gloom, not wanting to use her pocket torch but careful not to stumble or make a sound. She could feel Nellie's presence right behind her. Soon they saw a flicker of light ahead of them. Their feet made no sound on the path. The moon slipped from behind clouds, creating patches of silvery light in the woods.

Now they could see Burl Griffith, little more than a shadow up ahead. For someone with a bad leg and a limp, he moved fast. Samantha needed to stop and catch her breath, and she could hear Nellie breathing hard behind her, but she didn't want to lose sight of him. She was almost sure now that he was heading for the lean-to camp.

Suddenly, the camp came into view, and

Samantha realized that Mr. Griffith had halted. She stopped so abruptly that Nellie nearly tumbled into her. In the stillness, they heard Mr. Griffith call out quietly, "Silas? You there?"

Silas? Samantha's heart skipped a beat. *Mr. Griffith is talking to Silas Diffenbacher?* She saw Mr. Griffith move closer to the lean-to. The girls inched forward, then crouched behind some shrubs and cedar trees. Through the branches, they had a clear view of the camp. A tall, handsome man in a checked shirt stepped from the lean-to. Even in the shadowy light, Samantha could see that it was Mr. Diffenbacher. The dying coals of a campfire suggested that he had camped there overnight.

"Of course I'm here, you fool," he growled. "But not for long. I told you we shouldn't meet again for a while. It's too dangerous." Diffenbacher pulled on a leather jacket.

"You can't give up on buying the property," Mr. Griffith said. "You *promised* me land to build on."

Samantha squeezed Nellie's arm. Had

Diffenbacher promised to give Burl Griffith a piece of Grandmary's land?

"For your information, there won't be any property for you *or* for me if we don't persuade the old bat to sell, and so far she keeps saying no." Diffenbacher stepped back into the lean-to and came out again with what looked like a small valise. "And starting that fire last night— that was stupid. If the lodge had burned, and maybe the woods as well, the value of the property would have gone down. Way down." Diffenbacher appeared to be getting more and more angry as he talked to Mr. Griffith.

Samantha shivered. The Admiral had trusted Mr. Griffith, and Mr. Griffith had set the lodge on fire!

Mr. Griffith's voice was low and flat. "I was desperate. And I only meant to scare them. I couldn't think of anything else to do."

Anything else? Had Burl Griffith caused all the Piney Point accidents, trying to force Grandmary to sell?

"Okay, keep your mouth shut," Diffenbacher

said. "I'll come over to the lodge later this morning, make one last offer, and hope Mrs. Beemis has come to her senses."

Nellie pinched Samantha to say that they'd better slip away while they had a chance. As they turned to leave, Nellie stumbled, and a startled grouse flew up, wings whirring in the early-morning hush.

"What's that?" Diffenbacher shouted.

Samantha glanced back to see Burl Griffith moving toward them faster than she would have thought possible.

"Run, Nellie! Run!" Samantha whispered, pulling Nellie to her feet and making sure she wasn't hurt.

Samantha and Nellie ran, slipping and sliding on the pine needles that covered the path. The sound of pounding boots grew closer and closer behind them.

At last Samantha saw the lodge ahead of them, but no one was outside. She tried to call out, but she had no breath for even a whisper. She could hear Diffenbacher gaining on her and tried to run faster. As she passed the icehouse, Diffenbacher grabbed her jacket and hissed, "Open that door, Griffith!" He swung her around and shoved her forward.

She fell and slid across the cold floor, slamming into a block of ice. Nellie flew in right behind her, skidding into her back, jamming her even tighter against a wall of ice. Then she heard the thud of the heavy wooden bar falling into place across the door.

They were trapped!

14

A DROWNING RAT

Shivering all over, Samantha tried to catch her breath. The air she sucked in was cold, and musty with the smell of sawdust. Nellie shivered beside her. Samantha put both arms around Nellie. Darkness and an icy chill closed in around them, smothering them.

"Are you all right?" Samantha whispered, biting her lip to keep her teeth from chattering.

"I—I think so. What shall we do?" Nellie's voice wavered and Samantha knew she was trying not to cry. She wanted to cry herself, but what good would that do? *Think*, she told herself. *Wait.*

"I'm getting out of here," a muffled voice growled. It was Silas Diffenbacher, and Samantha thought he must still have been standing right by the icehouse door, waiting to see if he'd silenced them.

"Wait. Maybe—" Burl Griffith argued.

"You're a fool, Griffith. You've made a mess out of all my plans. Hey, what are you doing? Let me go."

"I'm not facing this alone," Mr. Griffith said. "You're going to stay and take half the blame. Or we can think of a good story."

Samantha heard the sounds of shuffling feet and fighting. Then a thud, and silence.

Even though the heavy door separated her and Nellie from the two men, she hardly dared breathe. She pulled her jacket closer, but the thin cloth did little to keep her warm. Her hands and feet felt like blocks of ice themselves.

"I think they're gone," Samantha said finally, helping Nellie to her feet. "Come on, we have to move." She tried the door, but it was firmly barred from the outside. She couldn't budge it.

Both girls pounded on the heavy door and yelled. "Help! Let us out of here!" they cried over and over. Then they stopped, leaning on the door to catch their breath. "It's no use," Nellie said. "No one can hear us."

Even with both their pocket torches, the icehouse was dark. The girls grew colder by the moment. "Try again," Samantha said, leaning on the door. "We can't give up. We'll freeze. Help! Someone please help!"

Suddenly, there was a scraping noise at the door. Samantha's heart banged against her ribs. Who was out there? Was it someone to help them—or was it Silas Diffenbacher or Burl Griffith? With a slow screech, the bar slid up and the door swung open. Homer stood outside, a puzzled look in his eyes. "How'd you get locked in there?" he asked.

"Never mind," Samantha replied. Beyond Homer, Samantha saw a welcome face. She grabbed Nellie's hand and ran out into the arms of the Admiral. He hugged them both tight, and Samantha practically collapsed with relief.

"Samantha, Nellie, we've been looking everywhere for you," the Admiral said. "Bridget came down and said that you and Nellie were gone. We've had everyone searching for you. Grandmary is frantic with worry."

Had that much time passed since they'd left? "I—I'm sorry, Admiral, but—"

"You're frozen. How on earth did you get locked in the icehouse?" The Admiral hugged her close again to help her stop shaking.

Grandmary hurried out the kitchen door and across the yard. "Oh, girls—look at you. Are you hurt?" Grandmary held out her arms and both Samantha and Nellie ran to her.

"Are they all right?" Arthur Porterfield and Trapper Jim came running around the lodge.

Samantha took a deep breath. "Mr. Griffith has been causing all the accidents, Admiral. He was doing it to help Silas Diffenbacher. Diffenbacher thought that if Grandmary got discouraged enough, she would sell."

"That can't be true," Homer burst out. He had been standing to the side, watching, after he'd let the girls out of the icehouse.

"How did you find this out, Samantha?" Grandmary asked.

Samantha looked at Nellie. They had to confess what they'd done.

"We followed Mr. Griffith through the woods this morning," Samantha began. "He went to the lean-to camp. Mr. Diffenbacher has been staying there. We overheard them arguing."

"When they found out we were listening," Nellie added, "they chased us back here and locked us in the icehouse."

The Admiral's eyes had turned steely. "Where *is* Griffith?" he asked. He turned to Homer. "Where's your father?"

As if in answer to his question, a sharp cry came from somewhere behind the icehouse, and then Jack's frightened voice called, "Help! Someone help me. Pa's hurt!"

The men ran toward the sound of Jack's voice. Samantha slipped from Grandmary's arms and followed. They found Jack bent over his father, trying to help him sit up.

"Where's Silas Diffenbacher, Mr. Griffith?" Samantha demanded.

Griffith moaned and held his hand to his

head. A knot swelled on the side. On the ground lay a heavy stick of firewood, surely the weapon that had been used against him.

"Leave Pa alone," Jack said. "Can't you see he's hurt?"

"I'm sorry, Jack," the Admiral replied. "We need your father to help us." The Admiral's voice was kind but firm.

"I don't know where Diffenbacher is," Griffith groaned. "He said he was leaving, and then he hit me." He lay back against Jack.

"I have an idea," Trapper Jim said quietly to Mr. Porterfield. "Come with me." The two men hurried down the hill toward the lake.

The Admiral got a length of rope from the shed and began to tie Mr. Griffith's hands.

"You can't do that to Pa," Jack protested.

"He has to, Jack," Samantha said. "Your father tried to set the lodge on fire. I think he caused a lot of trouble around here." She studied Burl Griffith's gray face. "Mr. Griffith, *you* damaged the porch step so that someone would fall. And then after Grandmary's accident, you hurried and put in a new step so that no one would see what you'd done. *You* put dirt in the pump, and you put the hole in the canoe, didn't you?"

Mr. Griffith didn't say a word. He just closed his eyes and turned his head away.

Glenda Griffith had come to see what all the fuss was about. "Oh, Burl," she said. She began to cry when she saw his tied hands. "What have you done?"

"I just wanted us to have our own piece of land," he muttered. He didn't meet her eyes. "I'm sorry, Glenda. I'm so sorry."

Samantha didn't want to cause Glenda any more pain, but she had to know the answer to another question. It was important. "Mr. Griffith, did Jack and Homer help you set that fire in the chimney? Did they help cause the other accidents?"

"No!" With an effort, Mr. Griffith lifted his head and looked straight at her, and then at the Admiral. "I swear they didn't have anything to do with this."

Was that true? Did neither boy know what

their father had been doing? Samantha studied both boys. Jack was kneeling beside his father, helping him sit up. Homer had his arm around his mother, about to cry himself. Suddenly, Samantha wanted to believe that they were innocent of all the trouble.

Grandmary pulled her shawl tight around her shoulders, her face grim. "Well, Samantha and Nellie, you girls took a big chance following these men. You shouldn't have done such a dangerous thing—but if you hadn't, both of them might have gotten away."

Glenda turned to Grandmary. "I'm so sorry, Mrs. Beemis, that my husband has caused all this trouble after you were so kind to give us a job. I'm so ashamed." Tears slid down her face. "Burl wasn't always a troublemaker. He changed after he went to war and got hurt."

Glenda took a deep breath and straightened her shoulders. "I know he'll have to answer for the grief he's caused you, Mrs. Beemis. I'll start packing. My boys and I will take tomorrow's ferry. We'll find work in the city."

A DROWNING RAT

Grandmary looked at the woman and her face softened. "You've been a good worker, Glenda. If you can promise me that you and the boys have had nothing to do with all these problems, you can stay on until I find a new manager."

Glenda looked at Homer and Jack. "We don't know nothing, Ma," Jack said. "Pa never told us anything about all this."

"That's right, Ma," Homer echoed. "We helped put out the fire, but we didn't know Pa started it."

Samantha looked at the boys, but neither looked at her. She hoped they were telling the truth. She'd give them the benefit of the doubt. She knew it was going to be hard for them to see the sheriff take their father away.

Just then, Mr. Porterfield and Jim came around the lodge. "Look at the drowning rat we caught, Mary," Mr. Porterfield said as he pushed a very wet and shivering Silas Diffenbacher ahead of them. His fancy mountain clothing clung to him, dripping water with every step.

"He tried to get away in the canoe," Jim

explained. "Fortunately, I hadn't had time to seal the crack in the bottom."

The Admiral's face held a huge grin. "Seems our rat can't swim."

Diffenbacher hung his head but stayed silent. He didn't need to confess, since Burl Griffith had done it for him. Samantha figured he would try to convince the sheriff that he'd had nothing to do with all the trouble at Piney Point, but trying to escape showed that he had.

"I suppose if these two gentlemen are tied up, they'll be secure in the tool shed until the sheriff arrives. Jim has volunteered to go to the village and bring him out here," the Admiral said. "But right now, I could use some breakfast. How about you, Mary?"

"I can't think of a better idea, Archie." Grandmary turned toward the lodge. She pulled Samantha close to walk beside her.

"Were you really going to sell Piney Point, Grandmary?" Samantha asked.

"I thought about it, Samantha," she replied. "But not for long."

"Mr. Diffenbacher couldn't persuade you?"

"No, he couldn't. And sitting on the porch with you, listening to the loons, remembering your grandfather and how we decided to buy Piney Point and make it a second home, I realized what this place means to me. I want to keep coming here as long as I can. Then I want you and Gard and Cornelia and your growing family to enjoy these woods and lakes. This is a special place."

Ooo–oooo, ooo–oooo. The voices of the loons floated up the hill to them. Their yodeling wails no longer seemed forlorn. The loons were happy in their watery home.

Samantha thought they, too, were saying that Piney Point was a special place. And she couldn't have agreed more.

LOOKING BACK

A PEEK INTO THE PAST

Grandmary's summer home at Piney Point is located in a beautiful wilderness region of northern New York State known as the *Adirondacks* (ad-uh-RON-daks).

The region's natural beauty has long attracted Americans eager to escape the bustle and heat of the cities. By the 1850s—long before Samantha was born—the region had become known as a place to vacation surrounded by fresh air, forested mountains, and abundant wildlife. The earliest vacationers were a mix of sportsmen, artists and writers, and wealthy tourists. Lodgings were scarce, so early vacationers

A loon chick rides on its mother's back.

often relied on local guides like the fictional Trapper Jim to help them camp, cook, and survive in the wilderness and to show them the best places to fish and hunt. These early campers often spent nights around the campfire telling tales as loons called out over area lakes.

By the 1870s, more and more visitors began coming to the Adirondacks, drawn by guidebooks and articles in magazines and newspapers. Railroads made travel to the region easier, too. Soon, large hotels catering to wealthy vacationers dotted the wilderness.

Early hunters and guides "roughed it" in the Adirondack wilderness.

MARQUETTE LAKE STEAMBOATS
MARION RIVER
to
KENWILLS.
Nº13
946

BLUE MOUNTAIN LAKE STEAMBOATS
BLUE MOUNTAIN LAKE
to
MARION RIVER CARRY
Nº13
946

By the late 1890s, ferries ran from train stops to hotels and homes in the Adirondacks.

To avoid the tourist crowds, some wealthy families purchased large tracts of land, where they established their own private "camps," just as Samantha's grandparents did at Piney Point. Many camps started as a collection of tents

for dining, sleeping, and entertaining. Gradually, the tents were replaced by log buildings and then by grand log homes. Wealthy families brought their servants from the city and enjoyed summers of comfort and leisure in the wilderness.

Soon, the Adirondacks became known as

an area where millionaires came to play in the woods. Some private camps even featured open-air bowling alleys, dance floors out over the lake, and Japanese-inspired interiors, complete with servants dressed in Japanese kimonos.

A land developer named W.W. Durant built many of the best-known camps in the Adirondacks. His clients included some of the wealthiest families of Samantha's time, such as the Morgans and the Vanderbilts. Their luxurious summer homes were often called "great camps."

In the early 1900s, Durant saw an opportunity to make even more

The main lodge at Great Camp Sagamore, built by W.W. Durant

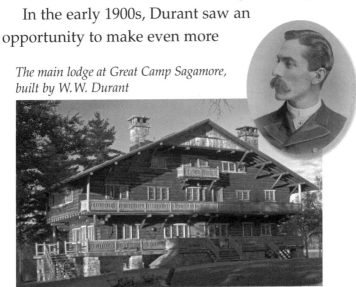

One of Durant's maps, showing small lots along a lake

money by dividing up portions of his lakefront land into smaller, more affordable lots. Durant hoped to sell the lots to middle-class people who wanted places of their own in the wilderness. Unfortunately for Durant, his questionable business deals and extravagant lifestyle caught up with him. His property and businesses were auctioned off to pay his debts, and his land empire crumbled.

As the Adirondacks grew more and more popular, some people worried that the area's beauty would be destroyed. Developers like Durant dredged channels for steamboats, dammed up streams, and cut down trees. Large-scale logging and other industries were also changing the Adirondack wilderness.

By the time Samantha was born, a vast Adirondack Park and Forest Preserve had been established to protect nearly three million acres of wilderness. Even so, development continued to threaten the region. Eventually, the New York state constitution was changed to include a special requirement that the Adirondack Forest Preserve would "be forever kept as wild forest lands." This provision gives the Adirondacks the toughest protection of any wilderness area in the nation.

Today, the Adirondack Park includes an area larger than the entire state of Massachusetts, and the region's beauty continues to appeal to visitors just as it did to Samantha and her family a century ago.

ABOUT THE AUTHOR

Barbara Steiner started writing stories and poetry when she was eight years old. Her favorite books were mysteries, and sometimes, all alone in a big house, she'd scare herself reading.

She has hiked and backpacked all over the world. She has ridden elephants in India and climbed into tombs in Egypt. She has claustrophobia but loves to explore caves. Her motto is, "Do something once a year that scares you."

She has published many books for children and young adults, including an American Girl History Mystery, *Mystery at Chilkoot Pass.* Her book *Ghost Cave*, set in her home state of Arkansas, was nominated for the Edgar Allan Poe Award for Best Children's Mystery. She now lives in Boulder, Colorado, with her three cats.